Loving the Texas Lawman

Loving the Texas Lawman

A Forever Texan Romance

Charlene Sands

TULE
PUBLISHING

Loving the Texas Lawman

Copyright © 2017 Charlene Sands
Tule Publishing First Printing, July 2017
The Tule Publishing Group, LLC

ALL RIGHTS RESERVED

No part of this book may be used or reproduced in any manner whatsoever without written permission except in the case of brief quotations embodied in critical articles and reviews.

This is a work of fiction. Names, characters, places, and incidents are products of the author's imagination or are used fictitiously. Any resemblance to actual events, locales, organizations, or persons, living or dead, is entirely coincidental.

ISBN: 978-1-946772-93-0

Chapter One

GRAVEL CRUNCHED UNDER Sheriff Jack Walker's boots as he exited his patrol car and headed for the cherry red sports car parked alongside the road just outside of Hope Wells. The Texas night sky twinkled above with bright stars, but on the ground his flashlight was his guide. Years of wearing a badge made him ready for anything and he knew better than to think he'd find a driver in that car, not with Wishing Wells, the town's natural flowing hot pool just fifty feet away. Lovers and others often frequented the waters past closing time, past curfew, sometimes breaking other Texas statutes as well. His mouth cocked up at the notion. He'd broken a law or two at the wells in his younger days. But Jack didn't rightly recognize the car and that put him on alert.

He crossed the road where gravel became wildflowers and then headed down the familiar path. As he came upon the gate, the chain link didn't appear to be jimmied, but that didn't mean much since the gate was more than climbable. There'd never been a need to secure Wishing Wells with anything more than a strong link fence, Hope Wells being a peaceable town for the most part.

The honeyed sweet scent of star jasmine flavored the air as he drew closer. His ears perked at a disturbance in the wells, a quiet swishing that only occurred when someone was upsetting the soothing waters.

"Who's there? You're trespassing at this hour. This is Sheriff Jack Walker." Giving fair enough warning for a trespasser, he climbed over the gate. He hoped like hell he wouldn't find two lovers going at it hot and heavy.

His flashlight illuminated the springs with a blast of brightness. Nope not two lovers at all, but one scantily clad woman.

A woman he recognized.

His eyes burned hot and his senses blurred.

He shined the light just below the soulful, baby blue eyes of the trespasser.

Damn.

Jillian Lane.

What was she doing here? He didn't think he'd ever see her again. It'd been years since Jillian had washed her hands of Hope Wells… and of him. He was over her, but cool and casual wasn't what pounded in his chest now. Instant disappointment at his reaction to her sent him back eleven years.

"Hello, Jack."

Her soft sultry voice filled him up with memories. "I see you're still breaking laws, Jillian."

A smile surfaced and the baby blues that had once done incredible things to him, seemed just as potent now. She had charm and grace to spare, a trait he'd once thought was exclusive only to him. He'd thought he'd known her mind too, but she'd proved him wrong in the end and his grief had lasted too long to admit, even to himself.

"As I recall, you helped me break more than a few, Jack."

The moonlit waters flowed freely around Jillian's bare shoulders. What in hell was the famous lingerie designer wearing underneath all that pooling water? A bikini? A thong? The woman ran a successful million-dollar company aptly named Barely There. Maybe Jillian wore next to nothing.

Jack drew a deep breath reminding him that Jillian wasn't the girl from the wrong side of the tracks anymore. She wasn't that poor misunderstood wild child that had once touched his heart and made him want to protect and cherish her. But seeing her at the wells again, unguarded, smiling up at him with a gleam in her eyes and that come-here look on her face, had him stumbling for a comeback.

She had moved on. So had he. Both had made something of themselves. It was best to let it alone. "Now I protect the law, Jillian."

She looked away, staring out into the darkness. "And the fine people of Hope Wells."

"One in the same."

She stroked the water, her hands playing over the pooling liquid like a delicate instrument. "You were meant to be sheriff. It suits you."

"Don't see as I could be anything else, what with my father and his father before him, being sheriff. It's in our blood, I suppose."

"It's a good thing, Jack. I understand you saved a little boy's life. You're the town hero."

"I'm no hero, Jillian."

His gut twisted. Visions of that fateful day tormented him still. That winter night six months ago, rain had poured down so heavily the banks couldn't hold and the river overflowed in large gulps. The blinding deluge and a set of bad tires had the driver of a sedan skidding off the road and plunging into the raging water. Trapped inside the car was a family of three, a young boy and his parents. Jack had seen it all happen from his patrol car and hadn't hesitated to jump into the river. Frantically, he'd searched for the passengers, hoping to help, hoping to save *everyone*. And then he'd seen it, the small arms of the boy flailing wildly from inside the car, his parents offering up the boy through the darkness as if to say, take him. *Take him*. Their faces strained in panic as they realized their fate. Jack would never forget that scene, as the swift current carried the car and the boy's parents under and away. There wasn't anything Jack could do for them but bring the boy to safety.

"I did what any other man would do in that situation."

"Not every man, Jack."

A breeze blew by and Jillian trembled. She'd been in the water too long. Typical Jillian. "I think it's time you got out."

"You mean I can't make a wish in the wells?"

"Is that what you're doing, wishing?"

She gave her head a tilt. "Maybe."

"It's cold tonight. You should get out."

"Is that an order, sheriff?" A teasing smile played on her lips.

"It's a firm suggestion."

"Will you hand me that towel over there?"

Jack reached for the towel hanging over a tree branch and walked closer to the wells as Jillian stepped out of the waters. Dewey droplets cascaded down her body adding a glimmering sheen on tanned, healthy-looking skin. He held the towel open, dipping his gaze to take a peek of frilly black silk covering her near naked body. *Male fantasy wet silk.*

"Thanks," she said, tucking herself into the towel.

"It's late. You'd best get to wherever you're going." He kept his focus on her face and off the tempting swells pushing the barriers of her towel.

"I've already been there," she said breathlessly, running a hand through wet hair, "and the Winslows weren't home."

Jack arched a brow, ignoring how the honey blonde strands fell against her bare shoulders. "You're staying at the Winslow place?"

"Yes. They said I'm welcome anytime."

Jack twisted his lips and shook his head. He had a thousand questions for her, but only one pounded hard in his head repeatedly. Why was she here? What brought her back to Hope Wells after all this time? "Damn, Jillian. As far as I know, they're gone for the weekend. Won't be back until Monday."

Jillian shrugged. "That's okay. I'll get a room at the motel or something."

Jack took his hat off and ran a hand through his hair. Leave it to Jillian not to see things through. She'd always been the impulsive one, the make-love-to-me now and damn the consequences, kind of girl. Jack had been the one to hold back, to want to wait, to do right by her. Jillian had been a temptation from the start, a girl he'd wanted above all else, but he'd been the responsible one. Sometimes, he hated that about himself.

"Doubtful. The rodeo's in town this weekend. You won't find a room anywhere."

Her face fell. "Oh."

She chewed on her lower lip and Jack's temperature rose watching her tongue dart in and out of her mouth as she contemplated her next move. He dragged his gaze off her mouth and glanced at his watch. It was almost eleven—too late for her to go traipsing along the highway looking for a place to stay. Jack doubted she'd find a vacancy for fifty miles or so.

Another breeze blew by and she shivered. Goosebumps

erupted on her arms as she hugged the towel tighter. Ah, hell. "Follow my patrol car. I know a place you can stay."

A nervous little laugh erupted and she shook her head. "No way, Jack. I'm not staying at the jail."

Jack didn't hide a wicked grin. "You don't have too many options, now do you? Get dressed. I'll wait for you by your car."

JILLIAN BOUNCED HER bottom on the bed, smoothing her hands over a soft cushy quilt. Jack hadn't taken her to jail after all, but instead led her to a residential house in the center of town. The tree-lined street and picket-fenced house was so… Jack. He'd surprised her when they'd walked past the main house and strode to this cozy guesthouse. The three, tiny rooms could probably fit inside Jillian's master bedroom back home in Newport Beach.

"This is wonderful, Jack. After the drive and the long time in the water, I'm beat. Can't wait to get into bed."

She glanced up to catch him staring. His dark expressive eyes latched on and didn't let go. Standing broad and tall, leaning against the doorjamb and looking gorgeous in his two-toned tan uniform—he'd been a hard one to leave behind. She'd halfway wished he'd become slovenly and overweight, making her decision not to come back to Hope Wells easier to bear. Instead he was better than she remembered. His granite jaw spoke of firm commitment. His wide mouth looked delicious and appealing. Day-old stubble only made him sexier, in that lawman kind of way.

Her body hummed with awareness, the boy she'd left behind had become quite a man. On warm, sultry California nights, she'd fantasize about young Jack Walker and what her life would have been like if she'd stayed in Hope Wells.

Even more, she'd wondered what Jack would be like as a lover.

Thanks to his sense of honor, they'd never gotten that far. Little did he know that his reluctance to make love to her, only gave credence to her innermost fears that she wasn't truly enough for him. Not tempting enough, not sweet enough, not desirable enough to make him lose his ingrained convictions and sense of righteousness for her.

The day she'd left Hope Wells, she'd cried a river of tears. Not for a town she wouldn't miss, but for a love that would go unanswered. She had left behind the one person in the world who had truly mattered, the one boy who believed in her, who had accepted and loved her despite a rather dubious upbringing.

But she'd never found her way back to Hope Wells. She'd never found her way back to Jack. No matter her success now, to the townsfolk she'd always be the wild child with the alcoholic mother. She'd always be the girl mothers warned their sons about. She'd always be the poverty-bound girl not quite good enough for honorable, steadfast Jack

Walker.

She hadn't come back to rekindle a relationship with her one-time love. No. That would be foolish. But her memories of him hadn't faded, as she'd hoped. If she made new memories with him, they too would linger and embrace her heart and touch her soul, long after she'd have to leave Hope Wells again.

"Sleep as long as you like. I've got some things to do tomorrow morning. You can stay the weekend."

His plans for tomorrow were exactly the reason she'd shown up here earlier than she'd planned. Breaking the news to him wouldn't be easy. But she had a problem that needed solving. And Jack might just be the only man to help her.

"Thank you, Jack. This place is great. Who used to live here?"

A scowl pulled his lips down. "My fiancée."

Something powerful slid through her heart as she thought of Jack having a fiancée. A woman he'd planned to spend the rest of his life with. When she'd spoken with Margaret Winslow last, she'd casually mentioned Jack's name. The woman told her Jack wasn't married, except to his job. He took his job as sheriff seriously. Everyone in Hope Wells respected Jack Walker.

"Oh?" She glanced around the place, suddenly noting how "female" the place looked from flowery curtains and cut-glass vases to softly plaid wing chairs. The tiny kitchen area, small living space and this welcoming bedroom spoke of a woman.

He cleared his throat. "She used the place as a studio. Spent most of her time here."

"Was she an artist?"

Jack shook his head, taking his time to answer. "Photographer."

Jillian nodded, seeing how this lovely space could inspire someone with talent. Then a thought struck. "Would I know her?"

Jack looked away clearly uncomfortable by her question.

Then he snapped his head back, his eyes sharp. "You could say that. I was engaged to Jolene Bradford."

Jolene Bradford? Otherwise known as Suzy Homemaker. Miss Virginity herself. The Girl Most Likely *Not* To. Jack had been engaged to the virtue queen of Hope Wells High. He'd planned to marry a woman so distinctly different and opposite than her that the contrast couldn't be second-guessed or denied. An odd sensation rippled its way down to her belly. She couldn't name it as jealousy, but perhaps envy. Envy that Jack had chosen a girl with a good family name, someone highly respected in the community, a girl that any man would be proud to take home to meet the folks.

"Can I ask what happened?"

"No."

Jillian nodded. Fair enough. She had no right to delve into his private life. It seemed Jack didn't care to rehash the past any more than she did, but she was curious why Jack hadn't questioned her more about her reasons for coming back. She would have thought a sheriff with investigative skills would've been more curious. But then, he'd find out everything he needed to know tomorrow.

Landing on his doorstep tonight hadn't been planned, but it sure made things easier. Remorse swirled in her gut along with a heavy dose of unsettling guilt. She had reworked all of her options in her head, argued with her business associates about it, but, in the end, this solution had become the most viable, most immediate, and most effective way of setting things to right. So when the time came, she had to ask Jack a huge favor.

And it was a whopper.

JACK REMOVED HIS gun belt and set it on the kitchen table. Twenty pounds of metal and leather lightened his load. He heaved a sigh and unbuttoned his shirt. With a flick of his wrist his shirt went flying onto the opposing chair. He grabbed a beer from his fridge and twisted off the cap. The brew cooled his throat and quenched his thirst. It didn't do much to ease his mind though, as his eyes honed in on a pile of legal documents waiting for him. He spread the papers out across the table and shook his head. He'd seen hundreds of documents in his profession, but this one meant something in his life. This one was personal. This one spelled disappointment, without so many words.

His chances for adopting Beau Riley were fifty-fifty at best.

Beau's hopeful, innocent face flashed in Jack's mind. When he'd pulled that little guy out of the river, Beau hadn't understood what was happening. He'd shivered and cried out of fear, but his heartbreaking loss hadn't been wholly evident yet.

Not until the rescue team arrived on the scene, offering little as way of hope. Beau's folks were gone. Jack had held the five-year old boy snug in his arms, rocking him in a soothing motion, keeping him warm, trying to fend off his fright. He'd tried to shelter the boy from the stunning blow by easing the truth out carefully. And once the boy grasped that his folks were gone forever, his quiet sobs had torn Jack's heart apart. The boy was an orphan now.

Single parent adoptions were difficult, even for the man responsible for saving the child's life. Jack had been forewarned. His chances weren't the best, but he had to try. What he had going was a solid sure reputation in Hope Wells. He had the town's respect, except for the abusers of justice, and he had family roots here going back nearly a century. What he didn't have was a stable home life. He didn't have a wife, someone to mother the child. Heck, he had no real prospects in that regard. And, at times, Jack thought to give up his quest for Beau, leaving him in the hands of the social workers to find a suitable family, a whole family, who would give the boy everything he needed.

Those heavy thoughts were outweighed by the memory of Beau clinging to him, his arms tight around Jack's neck, his small body trembling with fear.

Beau's innocent question seared Jack like a branding iron. "Who's gonna be my papa now?"

Now, Jack was the frightened one – afraid to lose someone else he had come to love. He had only been four years old when his own mother left town. The divorce knocked his world sideways and Monty had won full custody of Jack when his mother failed to show up to court. His father always said, it was for the best, and Jack had grown up being a loyal son to his dad, never really knowing his mother until she was on her deathbed. He'd gone to her then, as a boy of fourteen and held her hand during her last few hours on earth. She'd been a stranger to him, but his mother nonetheless. And Jack had shed tears at her passing.

The knock at the door startled him out of his thoughts. He glanced at the kitchen clock. It was almost midnight. He hadn't heard a car pull up so he ruled out his father, Monty, coming out for a late night visit. From the sound of the soft knock it wasn't his cousin Trey, who was most likely tucked around his wife Maddie at 2 Hope Ranch tonight. Which meant it could only be one person behind his door.

Jillian.

Lord, she was a complication he didn't need now. Jack approached the door with caution. Jillian was always up to something, forever getting in over her head. He wondered what it was this time. What in heaven brought her back to Texas after an eleven-year absence?

He opened the door and squinted, adjusting to the bright porch light. Jillian came into focus fast, standing on his doorstep wearing a delicate, crimson lace nightie. Shit. Blood pumped faster in his veins. The garment sported a tiny insignia BT on the scooped neckline – Barely There.

Hell, yeah. That much was true. There wasn't much material covering her body. Jillian had named her company appropriately.

He drew in a deep breath and waited.

"Jack." Her breathless voice and sexy outfit did a number on his brain. "This isn't what it looks like."

Chapter Two

"IT ISN'T?" JACK leaned against the doorjamb and shook his head slightly. "Now that's too darn bad, Jillian. Cause it sure looks… interesting."

Interesting? Since when was he a master of understatement? With her baby blues staring up at him, a man would have to be crazy not to like that package. But Jack wasn't crazy, just smart. He and Jillian were done and had been for a long time.

She crossed her arms over her chest, pushing up lush swells that nearly spilled out of her nightie. If she meant to cover herself up, the move was having the opposite effect, giving Jack a pretty enticing view.

Her face flushed almost the same crimson as that slip of material. "I remembered I needed to make a call and I couldn't find a phone in the guesthouse so I dashed to my car to get my cell phone and well, the wind blew the door shut. I'm locked out."

Jack twisted his mouth. Her explanation sounded reasonable and only a second passed before he realized he really did believe her. But maybe, just a small part of him wanted her to be standing on his doorstep for another reason, one that had to do with unrequited love and youthful regrets. Jack frowned at the thought before stashing it away. The last thing he needed right now was Jillian Lane, in any shape or form, regardless that her shape and form were in the drop-dead gorgeous category.

"Do you have a spare key?" she asked.

Jack nodded. "Come in. I'll try to hunt it down." He reached for her hand.

Just then the sound of footfalls caught his attention and the shrubs butting against his front yard fence rustled nosily. He darted a look outside. A man jumped out from behind a tree and a quick flash blasted light into Jack's face and then a camera began clicking away. Jack reached for his gun. It wasn't on his hip. On instinct, he yanked Jillian through the doorway and slammed the door shut. She stumbled to the floor and he went down with her, refusing to let her go. He covered her with his body.

If he was just a photographer, they weren't in mortal danger. Yet, Jack wasn't sure about anything right now, other than he had a soft, pliant woman under him and both were half naked.

He stared into wide blue eyes. "Are you okay?"

She nodded.

"Is someone after you? That guy ran away faster than a jack rabbit with a coyote on his tail."

Jillian wiggled a little under him. God. He took in every

soft curve, every subtle movement of her lithe body. It was torture. But he wasn't letting her up until he knew what was going on.

Jillian released a sigh and her breasts rose up to meet his chest. "Maybe."

Jack lifted himself slightly up and away from her heat, the sultry timbre of her voice and the soft curves addling his brain. "What does maybe mean?"

"I don't know who it was. But, lately, I've had photographers trying to shoot me. With a camera."

"Damn paparazzi. Stay here. I'll go check it out."

Jack rose and strode out the front door. In the distance, a car door slammed and an engine revved up. Before he could get off his front lawn, the car tore down the street. Whoever it was, they were gone.

Jack strode back inside the house to give Jillian a hand up, helping her to her feet. "Stay put, inside. I'm gonna check out the rest of my property."

He grabbed his gun and stepped outside, making a thorough assessment of the grounds; the side and backyard as well as the guesthouse. Satisfied no one else was trespassing, he returned to Jillian. "He must've gotten what he wanted and taken off. Jillian, are you being stalked?"

"Not exactly. Not in the conventional way. I suppose, I'm news right now. I, uh—"

Jack's phone buzzed. "Hang on. I've got to get this."

A minute later, he handed Jillian the spare key he'd

found in his junk drawer. "Sorry. I've got a call. Seems some of the rodeo riders got liquored up at Jinky's and they're giving the owner trouble. I've got to meet my deputy over there. Are you all right?"

Jillian nodded. "I'm fine. Really. This… has happened before. I'm not in any danger. They're just photographers out for a story."

What had Jillian gotten herself into? He didn't have time to question her. He took in her flushed face and reassuring smile. For a brief second, the young girl who had been taunted and teased for having no papa and a mama with a drinking problem, flashed in his mind. Jillian hadn't buckled under and her bravado had been the trait he'd been drawn to most. "Are you sure? You can stay here until I get back. I probably won't be too long."

"No, Jack," she said, lifting the spare key he'd given her. "I'll be fine in the guesthouse. Thanks."

Jack reached for his uniform shirt and jammed his arms through before strapping on his gun belt. Jillian's eyes stayed on him, watching his every move. Heat rose up his neck, the intimacy of this little scene not lost on him. He pointed his finger at her skimpy outfit, the haunting reminder of what she'd felt like under him, a recollection he'd not soon forget. "You'd better not go out looking like that."

He reached into his hall closet and handed her one of his old, plaid work shirts. "Put this on before you go outside again. And use the back door this time."

"Thanks." She worked her arms into the large sleeves and rolled them up.

His shirt hung on her loosely, sagging down to her knees. What should have eased his mind and cooled off his body had the opposite effect. Jillian looked cute, in a sex kitten sort of way and was seductive enough to make him shirk his duties tonight for more time with her.

"I've got to go."

Jillian nodded. "I'll let myself out."

Jack walked through the front door, keeping an eye out for any more intruders. Hell, one intruder in his life at a time was all he could take.

"Thanks again, Jack." Jillian called from his doorway.

Her gratitude wasn't for letting her stay in the guesthouse, or for offering her his shirt, but for caring enough to protect her just like he used to… when they'd been in love.

WEARING A PONYTAIL under her Texas Rangers baseball cap, sunglasses, and a pair of washed-out jeans, Jillian blended in with all the others in attendance at the Hope Wells Annual Rodeo Day. Yet the rodeo, which would be held later today, was only one of the day's many activities.

Set in a field in back of town, a picnic area included a small lake, where children raced their plastic boats. Makeshift wooden booths housed homemade crafts and game tables and large hand-painted signs tacked up on trees directed rodeo goers to the bake sale, bingo games, and contest arena.

Morning sun shined bright as Jillian stood in the background behind a column of trees, watching the proceedings from a short distance away. She kept herself secluded for just a moment longer, relishing the peace and tranquility that went hand in hand with small-town life. People mingled, children ran freely, laughter and lively conversation filled the air.

For the briefest of moments, Jillian wished she had become a real part of this town, satisfied by being a small-town girl, a wife, and mother who spent her Saturday nights at neighborhood potluck dinners and playing games with a houseful of children. But her life had taken a different path. She'd left small-town life for good, having been shunned by small minds and unsympathetic hearts. Ironically, now she needed Hope Wells and everything she'd worked so hard for banked on her making amends with the people here.

Jillian focused her attention on the raised plank stage in her direct line of vision. It wasn't hard to pick out Jack Walker in the lineup of uniformed men striding up the steps, ready to uphold the longtime tradition of raising money for local charities. Jack was everything a small-town woman would want in a man. Devilish good looks, a respectable job, and deep roots in this old ranching town. Bittersweet memories flooded her mind as she recalled all of the crazy dreams they'd shared.

But Jillian wasn't that young naïve girl anymore. She wasn't a small-town girl either. She'd found her home in a thriving, industrious city with work she loved. She'd been fortunate to find a mentor in the design business. A mentor, who'd believed in Jillian's talent and taken a young girl under her wing. Jillian had worked long hours, dedicating herself to her craft, giving her all to Missy Designs, headed up by Missy Eloise Sager. Missy had been firm, honest, and strict, but she'd also been a dear friend who'd shown Jillian the ropes in the heart of the Los Angeles garment district. Jillian garnered respect there and when Missy retired she'd encouraged her to branch off on her own, to start Barely There, Jillian's dream. And, after some time, she'd succeeded. She'd gained acceptance in the design world, acceptance that had eluded her in Hope Wells.

In those early years, Jack had written to her asking her to come back, telling her he'd missed her and asking if she was happy in the city. But she couldn't go back then. She was focused on her career. She loved design. She loved earning a living doing what she was meant to do. There were no such opportunities like that in Hope Wells. As much as she'd loved Jack, she needed to find herself, so she'd stopped writing him back. Stopped dreaming of him at night. Stopped longing for what was never to be.

Now, her eyes were on Jack as he peered out into the crowd. She knew him so well. She knew he hated all this attention, being in the limelight in front of a large gathering. Right now, he'd rather be anywhere else but here. But honorable Jack Walker wouldn't deny helping the charities. Maybe he'd see Jillian as a charity case too.

Jillian sucked in a breath, battling against old wounds and injuries done to her by this town. Maybe her image consultants were wrong. Maybe this wasn't the answer. Maybe she should pack it all up, and return home to the city.

A bout of loud tapping startled her. She glanced up to find Monty Walker, Jack's father pounding a gavel on the podium. The retired sheriff, graying at the temples, looking fierce and soft all at the same time, asked for attention. The older man had aged well and still commanded respect from the people he'd served in Hope Wells.

All eyes focused up, toward Monty Walker and the event about to take place. Monty introduced all the uniformed men on stage, five in all, with Jack garnering the loudest cheers. He'd always been the popular one, the boy with the bright future, the hero of the town now. It was Jillian's longtime association with Jack that had spurred this idea from the consultants who sought to save Jillian's company. They'd finally convinced her, but now, nothing seemed right.

With a loud rap of the gavel, Monty made the initial call. "Let the auction begin."

Jillian's heart raced. So much was banking on this.

Jack held a tight smile as the stream of shouted bids began for the *Sheriff for a Day,* the winner earning the opportunity to ride with Sheriff Jack Walker for one entire day.

Jillian waited and watched, stepping away from the tree that hid her identity. The bidding had gotten up to three hundred and fifty dollars, a sizable sum for small town pockets, until Jillian noticed who was doing the bidding.

Single, white, female, came to mind. *A stunning,* single, white female with a petite perfect body and a lush sheet of ink black hair. Jack made immediate eye contact with the woman and Jillian's heart hitched. An unfamiliar feeling clawed at her, as her thoughts took a different turn. She didn't know this woman. What was her relationship to Jack? Did he want her to win the bidding?

Jillian shook off those thoughts immediately, steering back on track and ignoring any internal warning signs. She'd come back to Hope Wells for one reason, and one reason only. Stepping further into the crowd, Jillian waited until the last possible moment.

Monty called out, "Going once, going twice—"

"Two thousand dollars."

Jack's head snapped in her direction, and he pierced her with a hard look that asked *what the hell are you up to now?* Jillian stared back at him, keeping steady, shoving aside her misgivings as undisguised gasps swirled around her. People moved aside making a wide circle as though she were a freak in a sideshow.

Then applause broke out, slowly at first and then a full

out round that thundered in the field. Monty squinted into the sun, narrowing his eyes until he finally recognized her. "Is that you, Jillian Lane? Well, doggone it, girl. You come up here on stage this very second."

Jillian moved forward, removing her hat and sunglasses. As her hair blew free, she smiled at Monty and climbed the steps heading for the podium. She walked past Jack standing next to the other deputies ignoring his long, questioning stare and put out a hand to Monty for a shake. The retired lawman grabbed her hand and tugged, drawing her to his chest in bear-like hug. To all it must have appeared a welcome reunion.

"What the hell is going on now, Jillie?" Monty whispered into her ear.

Thankfully, Monty's gruff tone was tempered with sincere concern. Jillian had never known exactly where she'd stood with Jack's father, but he'd always read her right. He knew her generous donation had strings.

Lord, she wished it wasn't the case.

"I need help, Monty. I'll explain later."

Monty pulled away enough to look into her eyes. A shaky smile emerged as she met his stare. He'd listen to what she had to say. Later, when the time was right. Monty Walker wasn't an easy man, but he'd gained a reputation through the years for being fair. Jillian banked on that, hoping he wouldn't tar and feather her before running her out of town.

After a brisk nod, he returned his attention to the audience. "This young lady has won the bid at... two thousand dollars." Monty glanced once more at her to confirm that he'd heard right. Jillian nodded. "Some of you might remember Jillian, a one-time resident of Hope Wells. She's made quite a success of herself in Los Angeles and well, heck, how many stores do you own now, Jillie?"

Heat crawled up her neck. Normally, she loved talking about her shops and never minded the attention.

Except, she sensed Jack glaring at her from behind, his displeasure coming through loud and clear. "Nineteen and I'm hoping to reach number twenty soon. Right here in Hope Wells."

The crowd was silent for a time then partial applause broke out. Jillian smiled tentatively, wondering if the townsfolk would welcome a trendsetting lingerie establishment set in the heart of Main Street. She took a tentative step away from the podium.

Monty grabbed hold of her arm gently, refusing to let her go. "Well, how do you like that, folks, one of those fancy girlie shops right here in town?" Monty continued on as if she'd simply stated she'd had eggs for breakfast. "Your generous bid will help a lot of people in this town. And you'll be sheriff for a day."

Her smile wobbled.

"Jack, you come on over here, son," Monty said. "And shake this girl's hand."

Jillian found herself sandwiched between the two lawmen, the younger, equally handsome one wearing a fierce expression. Jack's grip was firm on her hand but so exquisitely gentle, his heart-stopping touch made her squirm with guilt. She reminded herself some good would certainly come from her appearance back in town. She'd made a sizable donation for hospital and school charities, as well as bringing enterprise and jobs to the town when her shop opened.

Local newspapermen shouted questions as cameras snapped pictures of the threesome, Jack and Monty and Jillian. Monty faced the cameras with a wide grin, but Jack stood rigid, his body tense and taut. He refused to crack a smile. She needed to explain her situation to Jack and hope he would help her and, more importantly, she hoped he would forgive her for what she had to ask of him. She'd come here today for the positive publicity. She needed the good vibes.

And twenty minutes later, after giving an interview to the local reporters covering the event, Jillian fell onto a bench, mentally exhausted. She sipped from a water bottle and closed her eyes.

The bench creaked but the familiar voice didn't startle her. She'd expected Jack to seek her out. "You weren't kidding about the cameras, Jillian. Are you always being photographed?"

Jillian smiled despite Jack's dubious tone. "Only when I make news."

"This is hardly the news you're used to. Small-town stuff. Why'd you come, Jillian? The truth."

She nibbled on her lip and hesitated. She'd rehearsed her part well so many times in her head, but Jack's pensive stare did things to her train of thought.

She blurted, "My company's in trouble, Jack."

Jack leaned forward, his arms on his knees and he stared straight ahead, as if he didn't want to meet her eyes. "I know."

She blinked away her surprise and steadied her voice. "You know?"

"I ran a check on you last night. After that incident at the house, I figured something was up with you."

"What do you know, exactly?"

Jack turned to her, his dark gaze pinning her down. "That you got mixed up with the wrong guy. He turned out to be some sort of drug lord, and your company was implicated as a front for his business dealings. He was arrested and you barely escaped with your reputation in tact."

"I swear to you, I never knew anything about it. After what my mother went through with substance abuse, I'd never knowingly get mixed up with drugs or people selling them. But my company is suffering. I don't know how much more negative publicity it can withstand. Quarterly sales are way down and I needed to do something *positive*. It was suggested that I come back here to… to, uh—"

"Open a store. Throw your hometown a few bones,

make nice with the local charities."

"All of that, Jack. My image consultants believe this is the only way. But donating to charities isn't enough. I need backup. I need support from the right people. I need to be linked with, uh—"

Jillian dropped her gaze to his mouth. Lord, he had an appealing delicious mouth.

Jack blinked, his jaw tightening like a vice.

Her stomach ached so badly she could barely catch her breath. Jack was an intelligent man. Judging from the disgusted look on his face, he had to know what was coming next.

"With?" he asked.

Her shoulders slumped. She'd come this far and she had to see it through. She had to ask Jack this gigantic favor.

"With… you." The town hero, the most respectable, steadfast, honest man she knew.

He stood abruptly, hands on hips and stared at her for a long moment as if he couldn't believe her request. He shook his head firmly. "No way, Jillian. I won't be a part of your publicity stunt."

Jillian stood to face him, instantly regretting her wild scheme. Jack Walker was too forthright to engage in any form of deception. She'd been a fool to think so. "I'm sorry, Jack. I have a swarm of consultants breathing down my neck. They knew about you and your reputation here. It's a huge favor."

Jack spoke through tight lips. "Hell, Jillian. A favor is asking a friend for a ride home from work. A favor is helping your neighbor repair his broken down roof. What you're asking of me can cause a world of hurt."

"It wouldn't have to. We could work something out. Make it risk free."

Jack scoffed. "Nothing's risk free, Jillian."

He was right about that. Jillian had taken her share of risks in life, and most had panned out. But when they didn't, people did get hurt. The last thing she wanted was to hurt Jack again. "I understand. I'll get my things and move out first thing in the morning."

Jack nodded. "You going back to California?"

Jillian held her tears in check. None of this had worked out as she'd hoped. Jack wanted her gone. He probably hated her.

She shook her head. "No. I can't. I'm staying."

JACK WALKED AWAY from Jillian, his nerves ready to jump out of his skin. What she'd proposed was way out of line. Had city life changed her that much? Had the free-spirited young girl he'd grown up with become cold, ruthless, and calculating? Or was she that desperate to hold onto something she'd worked long and hard for? Jack understood hard work. He understood what Jillian must have sacrificed in order to become the success she was today. He also understood what her success had meant to her. She had come from a broken home and had struggled to hold her head up high, despite the cruel remarks aimed at the girl who lived on the wrong side of town.

Jack sighed, wishing Jillian hadn't returned to Hope Wells. She'd brought back too many memories… and too many promises. They flooded his mind and wrecked his conscience. *I'll always be there for you, Jillian. Whenever you need me.*

Was she banking on those vows spoken in his youth? Or had she forgotten? Hell, Jack couldn't figure out any of it, but he couldn't pretend to be in a relationship with Jillian. That spelled disaster. There had been too much between them, too much history and too much heartache. When her mother had ripped her away from her life here in Hope Wells, it hadn't been by Jillian's choice. But later, once she'd been freed of her mother's grasp, Jillian chose to stay away. She chose to stop answering his letters. She chose not to rekindle what they'd had. He'd made peace with it long ago. He'd gotten over her. Jack liked his life the way it was now.

His father, Monty, walked up holding Beau's hand. The five year old wore denim and a red plaid shirt, a size too small for him. The kid was growing out of his clothes. Jack made a mental note to put shopping for Beau on his list of things to do on his day off.

The boy's right cheek was painted with a blue and white

star that twinkled with some sort of glitter under the warm morning sun. As soon as Beau spotted Jack, he dropped Monty's hand and raced straight into Jack's arms. In a sweep, he lifted the boy and Beau's arms immediately wound around his neck, tightening the invisible bond they shared. Adopting little Beau would make a good life, even better.

"Hey, Buddy. Looks like you hit the face-painting booth already."

Beau turned his cheek for Jack's perusal. "It's the Texas star."

"I see that. Pretty cool."

"Yeah."

"Ready to have more fun?"

The boy nodded, his smile quick and eager. "Can we get a funnel cake?"

"I don't see why not."

"Great, my stomach's singing a hungry tune," his father said.

A young mother strolled by, holding her son's hand. Her husband wasn't far behind, packing a baby on his chest in some sort of nylon contraption.

"Afternoon," Jack said, giving her a nod.

The woman glanced at Beau clinging to Jack's neck. "It's sweet, isn't it?"

"Sure is." As they walked past, Jack was immediately seized by the normalcy of their family. One mother, one father and two children.

A sigh blew from his lips and he gazed at his father. Monty was shaking his head. "Don't go there, boy."

It wasn't the first time Jack was reminded that Beau would be better off with two parents, a mother and a father to raise him. But as his father, Monty, pointed out time and again, the boy had already formed an attachment to Jack. That much was true. And even his mule-headed father couldn't deny he'd fallen for little Beau as well. Monty had raised Jack after all, without benefit of a mother and he'd turned out okay. Monty had argued that Jack was a man he was proud to call son. It could be the same for Beau. They could make it work as a family, although, not exactly a traditional one.

"Hi." Dakota Jennings approached the three of them, aiming her gaze at the boy. "How are you today, Beau?"

"'Kay. We're getting funnel cakes."

"Oh, boy. I bet you can't wait."

He nodded.

"Do you think I can speak with Jack, just for a second? Is that okay?" She glanced at Jack, then at Monty and smiled.

Jack nodded. "That'd be fine."

"I won't be but a minute."

Jack lowered the boy to the ground and bent to look him directly in the eyes. "Why don't you two start walking over to the funnel cake booth? As soon as I talk to Dakota, I'll catch up with you. Won't be long, I promise." He ruffled Beau's hair.

"Come on. Let's get in that line before they run out of the dang things." Monty gestured for the boy.

Beau slid his hand into Monty's and they took off toward the festivities.

"Oh, Jack. He's adorable. Every time I see him, I think of what might've happened to him if you hadn't been driving by the river that day."

Jack winced. "I try not to think about that."

"Sorry for bringing it up." Her eyes softened. "I'm even sorrier that our little plan didn't work. Cole hardly noticed me, and he took off right after the bidding. I didn't even get a chance to speak with him."

Colby Ryan had issues, holding a secret only Jack was privy to and it was high time, in his estimation, his best friend dealt with those issues head on. Dakota was just the woman to help get Cole get on with his life. That girl had given herself a complete makeover to gain Cole's attention. Instead of a ponytail, her shiny black hair was styled in soft waves to the middle of her back. Makeup did just enough to showcase her beautiful green eyes and the tomboy horse wrangler of the Circle R Ranch was dressed in a summery dress that exposed loads of her sun-bathed skin. It'd been years since she'd showed a little leg. Most days she hid them under a pair of chaps or washed-out jeans.

She'd bid on Jack today to make Colby jealous. "You look beautiful, Day. Cole's nuts not to notice you."

Dakota lifted up to kiss him on the cheek. "Thanks, I

needed to hear that."

Jack drew her into his arms and hugged her tight. "Sure thing."

Poor kid. She'd been harboring feelings for Colby for a long time. Jack didn't pry too much and listened to Day when she had to get something off her chest. She was like a younger sister to him, and he'd gone along with her plan, because having Dakota as sheriff for the day would've been a breeze and if it helped her win Colby's attention it would've made her happy.

She stepped back to gaze into his eyes. "Let me know if I can help you with Beau, in any way. You deserve to be his father."

"Thanks."

"Oh and Jack? What's with that woman, Jillian Lane, coming back to Hope Wells? She outbid the hell out of me."

He shrugged. "Making a splashy entrance back to town, I suppose."

Her eyes narrowed on him. "Is there something between you two?"

Dakota didn't know much of his history with Jillian, leastwise, not anything he'd told her. "Nope." Not anymore.

"Good. One fool in love is all this town can handle."

"Gotcha. Want a funnel cake?"

"No thanks. You enjoy your day with Beau."

"Will do." And after she walked off, Jack hurried over to where Monty and Beau were standing in line. He slid in right next to them and took Beau's hand, peering down at him.

"Hey, Beau, you want one with strawberries?"

Beau shook his head. "Only lots and lots of sugar."

Monty laughed. "He'll be on a funnel cake high all afternoon."

"Nah," Jack said. "Won't be a problem."

Monty gestured toward the dirt parking lot off to the left, a cocky smile crinkling his lips. "Seems to me, you've got yourself a different kind of problem."

Jack followed the direction of his father's gaze. Jillian was behind the wheel of her sports car, revving up the engine. With sunglasses on and her hair tucked under her cotton Texans ball cap, she backed her car out of her space.

"What are you getting at, Pop?"

"I got eyes, boy. Jillian, she's a hard one to figure out, but I'd bet my badge the reason she's here has something to do with you."

"It does," Jack agreed, "but it's not going to happen. She's asking too much this time."

"And since when did you refuse that gal anything?"

Jack lifted Beau into his arms, so he could see the funnel cake batter being poured onto the griddle. "Starting right now. Hey, Beau, after we gobble the funnel cakes down, how'd you like a pony ride?"

"Yippee!"

He squeezed Beau gently and the boy's smile grew wider.

Jack put Jillian Lane out of his mind and concentrated on Beau and the two more hours he was allotted before having to return him to foster care.

Chapter Three

THE NEXT MORNING, Jack rapped his knuckles on Jillian's door, tamping down a wagonload of fury just waiting to be unharnessed. His patience dying, he fisted the morning newspaper with his other hand. "Jillian, damn it. Open the door."

It was early, but he didn't give a fig that he'd most likely be dragging Jillian out of bed. He didn't care that he made enough ruckus for two counties to hear. He had a mother of a headache and his nerves were rattled.

"The door's open," she called out.

It was all the invitation Jack needed. He shoved open the front door and strode inside. Jillian wasn't in the front room so he pressed on to the bedroom, unmindful of Jillian's privacy or state of undress. Instantly, he was hit by some flowery scent that only served to annoy him further. The small room steamed up with dewy mist wafting up from the bottom of the bathroom door. She was probably bathing. Great. He wouldn't allow his mind to go there, to think about her creamy skin lathered up with soapy bubbles.

A deluge of sexy garments were spread out across her

bed. Jack strode over to take a look of the pile of lingerie, his anger banked by curiosity. Plucking up one delicate, black satin thong with his index finger, he twirled the garment around. There was hardly enough material to comprise a pair of underwear. Jack bunched it up in his fist. Soft and lacy and delicate enough to rip easily. Jillian had obviously dreamed up, designed, and modeled this stuff.

Memories poured into his head of her stepping out of the waters at the Wishing Wells wearing nothing but black silk. And of how her skimpily clad body felt under him when he thought she was in danger the other night. Envisioning Jillian dressed in her lingerie occupied his mind and he cursed his traitorous body for reacting this way. He demanded more loyalty than that.

Jillian Lane *was* a problem. His head pounded even harder now. She could ruin everything he'd worked for up until this point.

"Jillian, will you get out here?"

"Hold your horses, Jack." Jillian came barreling out of the bathroom, her short white chenille robe partly open. Underneath, she wore a cream-colored cock teaser. At least that was what most men called it – a one-piece number cut high on the hips and low on the breasts, distinctly designed to drive a man completely insane.

Jack was part way there. He'd almost forgotten why he was pissed off. And what kind of turmoil Jillian had caused.

Jillian busied herself with tying the robe in place, as wet

tendrils of honey blonde hair fell onto her shoulders. Her face was scrubbed clean. She looked fresh, smelled like heaven and wore the tightly tied robe to distraction.

Jack stared for a moment. The pounding in his head moved lower to his heart, then further down to his…

He shook off his attraction. Jillian was upsetting all of his plans.

"Jack, I told you I would leave first thing. Are you here to toss me out personally?"

Jack's grip on the newspaper loosened. He unfolded the crinkled *Hope Wells Gazette* and tossed it onto the bed to face her. "You're not going anywhere, Jillian. We're both in deep trouble."

JILLIAN LIFTED THE newspaper and read the headlines. "Oh no."

Her heart in her throat, she lowered down onto the bed shell-shocked. This couldn't be happening. That damn photographer hiding in the bushes the first night she'd been here had snapped a photo of her and Jack on his doorstep. Apparently, the jerk had gotten exactly what he'd been looking for. The captioned picture of Jack inviting a scantily clad Jillian into his house suggested a late night booty call, a hookup with an old love. It didn't help that she'd been wearing a Valentine design that had been her biggest seller last February.

"Trouble Follows Jillian Lane Home." Jillian read silently, "Lingerie CEO and one time girlfriend to drug lord Enrique Vasquez, runs for cover to Hope Wells after allegations that her company, Barely There, posed as a front for Vasquez's illegal operations." She stopped reading. She knew the rest of the story. She'd seen enough similar articles written about her to fill up the *World Book of Jillian Lane's Mistakes*.

"Jack, none of this is true." She skimmed the article to the end where it finally stated that Jillian and her company had been cleared of all allegations and was no longer under suspicion. No formal charges had been filed. "It says so right here."

Jack stood above her, his stance rigid, unyielding. "I read the whole article."

"So why are you—"

"The picture, Jillian."

Jillian bit her lip and swallowed hard. "Yes, that was unfortunate."

"And the damn caption underneath."

Jillian peered at the bold writing. "Midnight Role Call for Hope Wells' Newest *Sheriff of the Day*. Jillian Lane caught taking lessons in Sheriff Walker's custody."

In true journalistic form, nothing in that caption could be deemed slander, but the innuendo was not to be missed. "Well, I guess no one would believe the truth."

"Hell, Jillian. *I'm* having trouble believing the truth. The damage is done." An unattractive snarl pulled at Jack's mouth. "Guess you got what you came for."

Jillian snapped her head up. "What do you mean?"

Jack glared at her. "You and me. Linked." He gestured toward the newspaper photo. "That's a very telling picture. It looks like, hell… it looks like I'm about ready to take you bed. And, damn, if you don't look willing. Wasn't that what you were aiming for? Upstanding sheriff hooks up with old flame. All is right with the world again."

"Oh!" She bounded off the bed so fast, the room spun as she skidded on a puddle of water, one leg sliding out in front of the other. Now was not the time to fall flat on her face. She yanked herself upright and struggled to maintain her balance, bubbling with righteous fury and stabbing a finger into Jack's granite chest. "You can't possibly think I *arranged* for that picture to be taken. You can't possibly think that I'd want to be associated with you like that. You can't possibly think for one doggone minute that running around in my Valentine Vamp and having the world think I slept with you, could be good for my image."

Jillian squeezed her eyes shut and contemplated a long moment. Silently she called him every four-letter word in her vast vocabulary and then some.

"Valentine *Vamp*?"

She removed the finger poking his chest and stepped back, giving him her chin. "My best seller so far."

"I can see why. You cut way down on material costs."

Jillian inhaled sharply. Jack had always been quick on the uptake. He used to make her laugh until her belly ached. Now it ached for quite another reason.

Defending her livelihood and her company would always be her first priority. Barely There was her *baby*. The only family she had left. Her mother had passed on last year. "You didn't seem to mind the other night. It took you less than a second to jump on top of me."

He'd felt so very good on top of her. His long legs pressed against hers, his raw male scent enveloping her, his arms protective and tight around her. She'd never admit it to a soul, but every second in Jack's arms felt like heaven.

"To protect you, damn it."

Jack eyes darkened and his nostrils flared. She'd managed to piss off a man that never really lost his cool.

Jack was always in control, always rational. That trait made him the man he was today, but so often in the past Jillian had wished he would cut loose. She wished he'd walk on the wild side once just for the experience. Just to know that he had.

But Jillian conceded the point. She'd taken an unfair shot at a man who truly wanted to protect her. "I know. Jack, listen to me, I didn't know that sleazy photographer was out there. I didn't plan to knock on your door that night. I really was locked out. None of what happened was arranged."

Jack paced the room deep in thought. Jillian stood against the wall, arms braced behind her, watching, waiting. Finally, he came to stand in front of her, his eyes softening, his stance more relaxed than she'd seen him. "Okay."

"Okay?"

"Yeah, there's nothing to be done about it. The whole town's going to think we're sleeping together now. Not the image either of us wants."

The stab cut through her heart. She shifted her gaze away from him and his wounding words. "Am I that b-bad for your reputation?" It was as if she'd been cast back in time. She was that young girl again, not quite good enough for Jack Walker. She was back to being someone who could only cause him trouble.

"Hell no, Jillian. But this isn't about me anymore."

"Is it about that woman who kept bidding on you yesterday?"

The three of them had looked so perfect together—Jack, the little boy and the woman. Jack seemed to have real affection for her and it killed her to think so, but Jillian didn't have any rights when it came to Jack Walker. She had no claims on him. In her mind, he was as off-limits as stolen lingerie designs. Jillian had chosen her path in life.

But there were times, too many recently, when she wondered about her decision to pursue her career. She wondered if she'd stayed, could she have seamed together a life with Jack Walker, making babies, enjoying Sunday afternoon cookouts and rooting herself deep into Hope Wells?

"No." Jack scoffed, shaking his head. "It's not about her. She's not my girl."

"Could've fooled me." It was impossible to keep her voice light.

"Jealous?"

She had been. Foolishly. Ridiculously. Incredibly jealous of the woman Jack had taken in his arms and kissed under a mesquite tree.

She refused Jack an answer. "We were talking about reputations. You said this wasn't about you anymore. And if it's not about her, then what is it about?"

Jack filled his lungs and walked to the quarter-paned window to stare out. A beat, and then another passed.

Finally, he spun around and met her eyes. "It's about me adopting little Beau Riley. It's about me walking a thin line in order to qualify for a single parent adoption. It's about me being the best option for the boy."

Air deflated from her lungs. "Oh, Jack."

She hadn't expected this. Not from Jack. He was usually easy to read. There were never great surprises with Jack Walker. But this time, he had surprised her. She'd never seen such passion or determination in Jack's eyes before. He clearly loved that little boy he'd rescued. No doubt Jack would make an incredible father. And now she might have destroyed his plans. "Do you think your chances are ruined?"

"Could be. After seeing that picture, who'd believe we

weren't having an affair? From the social worker's point of view, how eligible does that make me? What kind of environment would I be subjecting the boy to—a bachelor with an active sex life?"

"Jack, your reputation is impeccable."

"Professionally, maybe. But my personal life won't win any awards. I've had my share of… never mind. Then my live-in fiancée left me and now it appears I'm having midnight bootie calls with an old girlfriend."

Jillian's teeth dug into her bottom lip as she searched for answers. How could she get Jack out of this? She was drawing a blank in the get-your-ex-out-of-this-mess department. It was frustrating as hell. Her only option was to leave and hope it all blew over.

She lifted her Gucci suitcase from the floor and plopped it onto the bed, unzipping the bag with a quick slide of the wrist. Carelessly, she began tossing her lingerie in. "I'm so sorry, Jack. I'll be out of here pronto." She turned to him holding back a well of tears.

She'd been self-absorbed and concerned by her own needs and hadn't allowed room to consider anyone else's problems. "I never meant to hurt you. Not back then. Not now. I don't want to cause you any more trouble. You have to know if there was any way I could fix this, I would."

JACK INHALED A sharp breath. This had all happened within a blink of an eye. He didn't know for sure his chances were ruined, but he'd always gotten the impression that Mrs. Givens was a traditionalist, believing in the sanctity of marriage, especially when it came to adoptions. The only thing Jack had in his favor with the social worker was his status in town as being a fair and honest man. Maybe he could explain the truth to Mrs. Givens. Maybe, she'd understand the situation and recommend him for adoption. If she didn't, another couple was most likely waiting in line, a man and a woman, who'd adopt Beau instantly if given the chance. He'd lose Beau for good. How could he explain to the young boy, he couldn't be his father? How could he disappoint the boy who had come to rely on him? And how could Jack lose yet another person in his life he had come to love?

Jack stood rooted to the spot contemplating. It was only when Jillian touched his hand, depositing the cottage key into his palm that he realized she was dressed, her suitcase was packed and she was ready to walk out of his life. Again.

He watched her throat move up and down as she took a deep swallow. Her hair had dried into long honeyed waves catching the morning light and caressing her shoulders. She wore a short, scooped-neck flowery dress and tall sandals that seemed to defy gravity. No doubt she wore matching underthings too, something she designed. Something that would make a man's breath hitch and his groin tighten. She was beautiful and dangerous. She was better off long gone.

"Good-bye, Jack." True regret rang on each syllable.

When he didn't respond, Jillian hoisted her suitcase and walked toward the bedroom door. There wasn't much else to say, was there? This was for the best. Her hand reached for the knob.

A crazy thought hurried to his brain. *If there was any way to fix this, I would.*

"Did you mean it, Jillian?" he asked quietly.

"Mean what?" she said, making a half turn and settling her baby blues on his.

"That you'd help me fix this if you could?"

"I meant it."

"Then don't leave."

"You w-want me to s-stay?" Jillian's voice cracked and she turned to face him fully.

His mouth cocked up as he gave her a nod. "Stay... and marry me."

The suitcase dropped from her hand. Plunk.

She stared at him as blood drained from her face. Her eyes were big blue circles against a pale canvas. *Yeah, that's right...* Jack Walker knew how to charm a lady. His offhand proposal got his point across, sparing no amount of sentiment. He was doing this for Beau. And for Beau's parents.

Take him.

He'd do anything to gain custody of the boy. Including marrying her.

Wasn't that what she wanted anyway? To restore her good name and reputation? To keep her precious company afloat? Getting married would solve both of their problems.

"You want me to marry you?"

His throat closed up. Was this really happening? Had he just proposed to Jillian? A dozen doubts crept into his head. It was a fool notion, but he didn't see any other option. If Jillian agreed and that was a big "if", somehow he'd make it work. "That's what I said."

Her gaze shifted away. She was gone, lost in thought, standing there, half in, half out of the room. An annoying twitch poked at his jaw. He held his breath and didn't know if a yes or a no answer would break him out in a sweat.

Finally, her eyes lifted to his. "When?"

"The sooner the better."

Chapter Four

"It's nuts, you know," Jillian said.

Of all the crazy things she'd wanted from Jack, a hurried loveless marriage proposal wasn't one of them.

"I know." Jack lowered onto the bed and spread his legs wide. Resting his elbows on his knees, he dipped his head and stroked his palms down his cheeks. His lips parted in a sigh and his weariness echoed in her ears. "Nutty enough to work."

She walked toward the bed and sat down on her knees on the floor facing him, tucking her feet under her butt. Once upon a time, they'd sit this way dreaming of their future. Only now, Jack wasn't cradling her head and whispering words of love.

"Is it what you want?" she asked.

His eyes brimmed with the truth. "What I want is to adopt Beau."

Dear Jack. He was always doing the right thing. She couldn't fault him for wanting to help the boy. "There's no guarantee if I marry you, that you'll get custody of the boy, is there?"

"I'd have a better chance. Are you trying to back out?"

"I didn't say that."

"If we got engaged right away, it would serve to undo most of the negative effect of the newspaper article. We'll throw a big party for our engagement. We'll convince everyone we've fallen in love again. They should buy that. There are a lot of people in town who still remember that we once dated. We'd make it seem real."

"You're willing to use deception?" Deep down, she blamed herself for that transgression too, putting him in the position to deceive just about everyone he knew.

He gave a quick nod and his lack of hesitation told her how very much he wanted to adopt Beau Riley and become his father. Jack didn't lie. Well, maybe only to himself, but Jillian could never convince him of that, back in the day. When he'd told her he wanted to be with her no matter what, Jillian thought he'd believed it in his heart. But leaving town and not following his path in life, not becoming Sheriff Jack Walker, wouldn't have suited him. Jillian had been smart enough to know that.

"Isn't that what you've always wanted? For me to act on my wild side? For me to do something crazy. Well, I'm offering crazy."

So, marrying her would be wild and crazy? He'd never know how much that stung. Even she had to admit the situation was a catch twenty-two. Both would get what they wanted, but somehow it all seemed unsettling and disingenuous and she'd have to live with the fact that coming back to town had caused this mess. "You love Beau that much?"

He didn't reply and really there was no need. The answer was incredibly obvious judging by what he was willing to do for the boy.

"If it goes through, the adoption finalizes in a year," he said. "That's all I'm asking of you."

"A year?" Jack put a time limit on their fake marriage? Jillian's heart seized up.

She'd never been engaged before and, luckily for her, her relationship with Enrique hadn't progressed that far before his family's illegal dealings came to light. Now, with the *Gazette* headlines upfront and personal, the fine folks of Hope Wells had that to hold over her head too. They'd think her guilty by association, just like everyone else. And nod their heads in agreement, deeming their first opinion of her correct. She was nothing but a wayward girl gone wrong. When it came time to end her marriage, she imagined the entire town would rejoice. Good riddance to Jillian Lane. Jack would be better off without her. It would be just one more notch to scratch on their bedpost of indiscretions about her.

She'd once thought a marriage proposal coming from Jack Walker would be nothing short of heaven-sent. Oh, how wrong she'd been. But there was one person they weren't fully considering. "What about Beau? Wouldn't I be his…his mother?"

Doubt immediately crept into Jack's eyes. It was clear he hadn't thought this entirely through. He was so determined to give the boy a home that he hadn't considered that Beau could actually become attached to her.

After a moment, his expression transformed and he pushed air out of his lungs. "I expect you'd be gone a lot. Working. It's what you do, right?"

He was clear as a bell. He didn't want her around. The less time she spent with them, the less misery she'd cause. Okay, she got that. It was a knife twisting into her heart, but she understood his reasoning. Jack was protecting the boy from future heartache. Still, the jab went deep.

"Yes…that's true. But what if Beau doesn't like me?"

Jack shook his head in a familiar way. He'd never believed anyone wouldn't like her once they got to know her.

Mrs. Jeffries sneered at me again when I was buying groceries.

Billy Springer tripped me on purpose outside the diner.

Loretta Woodburn laughed at my patched jacket in study hall.

She would confide in Jack her innermost feelings and he'd find a way to make her feel better about herself. Mrs. Jeffries had a permanent disfigurement and looked at everyone that way. Billy Springer was clumsy as an ox. Loretta had a nervous giggle she couldn't contain. Drove everyone batty.

Jack saw the good in people. Even her, once upon a time.

"Beau likes *me*," Jack said. "That has to be enough for now."

Oh. Sweeping sadness struck her like a blunt blow to the heart. Jack wasn't going to console her and make her feel better this time. He wasn't going to find a positive to her negative. He wasn't going to make her bumpy road smooth again.

She'd lost something very special with him. Something she'd never regain and how very heartbreaking that was.

Years ago, she'd blamed her mom for everything bad in her life, especially her father's leaving them behind to fend for themselves. Much later, she'd learned the truth. Her father had been a miserable, verbally abusive man. And her mother's drinking problem stemmed from his abandonment. Jillian had been too young to see it then. Her mom had loved her, but she certainly wasn't mother of the year. Not by a long shot. There were times when Jillian hated her for being the town drunk, for her lack of mothering skills, for never putting her daughter above her need for the next drink.

Shame had become ingrained in Jillian's soul, etched so deeply she couldn't purge it out. When she'd left Hope Wells, the weighty burden had been lifted from her shoulders. She'd been freed. She could start fresh. The world was hers for the taking. No one knew her business. Her family life was private. She didn't have to feel ashamed of her mother. Jillian Lane was just one more gal trying to hit it big in the city.

Leaving Jack behind had been her only regret. She'd left him along with all of her other baggage. The best thing she could do for him now would be to run out again. Leave town and never come back. But he wanted the boy and, somehow, she owed him that.

But how could she assume the delicate role of mother to an orphaned boy? She wasn't exactly cut out for motherhood. She had plans that didn't include a little boy and a man who could barely stand her. A man who held her responsible for his heartache years ago and blamed her for ruining his chances of adopting Beau now.

After her disastrous love affair with Enrique, she'd pretty much sworn off men. But that didn't stop her from coming to Hope Wells, to use Jack and his good reputation for her own gain.

"It's just that I'm not sure I'm the best candidate for the job."

"Job?" Jack scratched his neck. "Well now, being as you're the only other person in that newspaper photo, Jillian, I don't think I can switch out another woman to replace you."

She put her head down and stared at the ground. Jack was right. He couldn't very well introduce another woman as a love interest and possible marriage prospect with that telling picture of them splashed across the front page.

"I'll do it," she said. Heaven help her, she was digging

herself into another hole. "I'll marry you… but I have a few conditions."

AS THE SUN dipped on the horizon, a magenta sky cast a sheet of warm color over the land. Jack liked this time of the year best, when the sun's descent hinted at cooler air and dark shadows of dusk. He parked his patrol car alongside his cousin Trey's house and removed his sunglasses. Standing firm on 2 Hope Ranch soil, he took a solid breath and glanced around the prosperous, but humble ranch his cousin had managed to save. Horses whinnied from the stables and the familiar scent of cowhide and leather made its way to Jack's nose. He didn't mind the smell some considered god-awful. He wasn't a stranger to ranch living. Though he'd always lived in the residential part of town, most of his friends as well as Trey were ranchers.

He climbed the steps and knocked. Maddie, Trey's wife, opened the door. Her face flushed and her eyes twinkling, she greeted him wearing a bubblegum pink apron and a sweet smile. "Hey, Jack. How're you doing?"

"The real question is, how're you doing?"

She landed a delicate hand on her belly. The bump was just about noticeable now and Jack grinned every time he saw it.

"We're just doing. All three of us are happy as clams. I'm

glad you stopped by." She stepped back and allowed him entrance to the house.

That was what he loved about Maddie, her genuine grace and a down-to-earth quality that invited friendship. She was an amazing woman and Trey had been smart not to let her walk out his life. Jack liked to think he had a hand in keeping his cousin from making a colossal mistake in letting her go.

"Is Trey home? I sorta need to speak to both of you."

"He just came in for the day. He'll be out of the shower soon. I'm making chili. You'll stay for dinner, right?"

"If that's your delicious cornbread I'm smelling, I'm staying."

He followed her into the kitchen and just like that, she cut a corner of the yellow flat-pan bread and handed it to him. Immediately, a napkin appeared under his chin. Jack took a huge bite. "Oh, man." He chewed and then wiped crumbs from his mouth.

She grinned. "Wanna beer to wash it down?"

He scrubbed his jaw. A six-pack would do him better. "Sure. But I'll get it. You don't need to be serving me. Sit down and take a rest." Jack grabbed a beer and a pitcher of lemonade for her and shouldered the fridge door closed.

She laughed. "Jack, I'm only four months along. I caught a filly today out at Weberly's farm. Poor Maisey had a time dropping her. The girl needed some help, which also makes me perfectly capable of fetching you a drink."

He opened a few cupboards until he found a Mason jar glass and brought it to the table. "All the more reason for you to rest, you worked hard today."

"Doing what I love, is hardly work," she announced.

She'd probably gotten the same kind of hovering and protective treatment from Trey, so Jack got the message loud and clear. He'd back off. Maddie was a smart woman and a damn good veterinarian, specializing in farm and equine medicine. She had an office in town, but lately, due to Trey's insistence she'd been working more from the ranch.

"Is that my pain-in-the-neck cousin I hear?" Trey sauntered into the room and tossed his arms in the sleeves of a fresh chambray shirt.

Maddie's pretty green eyes immediately lit on him and the love that poured over her expression struck Jack like a hammer to the chest. He envied their relationship, but never once resented it. It was just that he hadn't found a woman that made him dizzy and crazy and silly in equal parts. A woman who filled all the holes and gaps in his life, the way Maddie did for Trey.

He'd never had a woman look at him like that either… not since Jillian Lane. All those painful years ago.

That relationship had been wrong from the get-go. It had taken Jack years to get over her. He wasn't thrilled to be thrown back in the arena with her, but what choice did he now have?

Trey strode over to him and they shook hands. "Hey,

Jack."

Maddie handed him a beer and pressed her lips to his cheek as he sat down at the oval table to face him. As Maddie moved away, Trey reached for her catching his wife in his grasp apparently wanting more than a little peck, but she was quick to wiggle out of his arms shaking her head. "Oh, no you don't, Trey Walker. You're not gonna make me burn another dinner. We've got company tonight."

"Sounds like an everyday occurrence," Jack said. "Maybe I should leave, so you two can get to burning more meals."

Trey's gaze lingered on his wife.

Maddie pretended not to notice. "Don't be silly, Jack. We're happy to have your company." She turned to the chili pot.

Jack scratched an imaginary itch under his jawbone. "Yeah, about that… me showing up here unannounced."

Trey took a swig of beer. "Nothing new there."

"Today, something's new. And I'm about ready to bust a gut if I don't tell you."

Maddie stopped stirring chili and swiveled around from the stovetop, her eyes wide and curious, the wooden spatula in her hand dangling precariously over the pot.

"Oh yeah?" Trey stretched out his long legs and balanced the chair on its back legs. Rocking slightly, he brought the beer bottle to his lips again. "What's that?"

"I'm getting engaged."

Trey's chair thudded forward and thumped, putting the

exclamation point on his message.

Maddie gasped. "What in the world?"

Jack expected their stunned reaction. He hadn't dated a woman in months and there hadn't been anyone special for a long while. "In case you haven't guessed. It's Jillian."

"You're going to marry Jillian Lane?" Trey's voice rising to an uneven pitch gnawed at his nerves.

"Before you jump to any conclusions, wrong or otherwise, let me explain."

He spent the next few minutes, laying out the events that had led up to his decision to ask for Jillian's hand in marriage. He told them how they'd reconnected instantly when she returned to town, realizing their feelings for each other hadn't died. The unfortunate photograph and news article that had come out had put them both at a disadvantage. Jillian needed stability in her life and Jack wanted to adopt Beau. Together, they'd agreed that getting married quickly would help them attain both. Why wait, was how he put it.

He never mentioned love, or the temporary part of their arrangement, which was weird because he'd had every intention of telling his cousins the entire truth. But once he began speaking, those words refused to come and he knew damn well why. It was hard enough admitting it to himself, much less to the cousin he thought of as a brother. Because if Jack was one thing, he was honest and using deceptive means to gain his objective wasn't in his wheelhouse. Under normal circumstances it wasn't something Sheriff Jack Walker would ever consider doing, but this wasn't an every day, run-of-the-mill kind of engagement.

Both of them had something to gain by speaking vows. Both wanted something out of the union. Jillian needed a way to earn back the trust of her clientele and rebrand her tarnished image and, of course, he wanted to adopt Beau. Their marriage would be a fraud. What they were doing was pure damage control. He felt like crap deceiving the ones closest to him. But still the words would not come. Guilt washed over him. When had he become such a damn coward?

"Wow," Maddie said. "Congratulations. I guess I'll have to invite Jillian over to get to better acquainted with her. She's going to be family soon."

Ah hell. He was a first class heel. Jack tugged on his ear and then gave her a nod. "Yeah, that'd be real nice."

"I always knew you two would find your way back to each other." Trey grinned, in that I-told-you so manner that left Jack gnashing his teeth. "Even if it is to quench the thirst of the prying press… among other things. You two will give Beau a loving home."

"How can you be so sure? You never gave Jillian a chance back then. You weren't too keen on her, as I recall."

Trey shrugged and glanced at his wife. Maddie possessed his heart and had turned his world upside down in the best way possible. "You're forgetting that I didn't think anyone could wind up happily married. Not after all the marriages and divorces Dad had. I almost let my father's dying words destroy my life."

The scent of saucy meat and hot spices wafted to his nose as Jillian began dishing up the chili. "The Walker curse that never was," Jack muttered. "Glad you wised up."

"Me too," Maddie said, coming to the table balancing two steaming hot bowls in her hands.

"Me three." Though Trey hated admitting he was wrong about anything, he was man enough to know he'd almost blown it with Maddie.

"Here, let me help you with that, sweetheart," Trey stood, taking the bowls from her hands and setting them down. He helped transfer the cornbread to the table and waited for Maddie to take a seat.

"Are you saying you weren't opposed to me and Jillian?" Jack asked.

Trey nodded. "That's exactly what I'm saying. I had nothing against her or her mother. It was sort of sad if you ask me, with Jillian's father running out on them. And the whole town thinking of them as trash."

Jack's eye twitched. A sigh blew from his lungs.

Trey noticed. "I can see it in your eyes now, Jack. You looked fit to be tied. You've always had strong feelings for her, but this is happening real fast. I only hope you're sure about what you're doing."

"I'm sure."

He was. About Beau. His heart and his brain told him

they were a good match. They'd be father and son and that would be that.

"Then I'm happy for you. When's the wedding?"

Jack sipped his beer slowly and then took his time to plunk the bottle down. "You'll know as soon as I do."

"It's lovely, Jack."

The engagement ring slid easily onto her finger, the round multifaceted three-fourths of a carat diamond reflected light in a tasteful gold setting. Jack shouldn't have gone to the expense and she had every intention of returning the ring, after…

She was keenly aware that this gem wasn't his grandmother's diamond ring. The family heirloom he'd talked about giving her one day, the one that had adorned his mother's hand and her mother, before that. She didn't expect it, after all. That pear-shaped diamond surrounded by a cluster of baguettes was meant for permanence, not pretense. That ring was meant for the woman who would hold his heart into eternity.

She gulped air. Had he given that ring to Jolene Bradford?

"I'm glad it fits." He stepped away but there was only so far he could go in her tiny kitchenette. It was midnight and she hadn't expected him to come over so late. His text had said it was important.

Important and *life-changing.* So here he was standing tall and dutiful in his crisp tan uniform, his eyes riveted on her, as if calculating the next step in his plan.

Her fiancé.

"I suppose we should make the announcement soon," he said. "Have a party… or something."

Jack hated having attention thrown at him. He was at peace being a jester, teasing others and making them the center of attention. Jack Walker, for all his snark and wit, was really a pretty humble guy.

"We'll do both. I'll be happy to take care of it, if you'd like." She'd thrown more than her share of parties. Coming up the ranks in Los Angeles, she'd been privy to helping Missy plan parties for the rich and fabulous. Hosting a small-town engagement party would be child's play for her.

He nodded. "Yeah, thanks."

"Would you like a glass of wine or some champagne to celebrate?"

He turned his wrist, barely glancing at his watch. "Uh, I've got an early call in the morning."

"I see. Are you going to your own execution?" She tilted her head and smiled sweetly.

He snapped his eyes to hers and she held his stare, raising her brows.

"Jack, no one's gonna believe we're engaged if you go around sulking all day. You've got to act the part."

His gaze dropped then, heating a trail along the line of her plush short robe to her bare legs. Her toes wiggled in response and his mouth twitched at her cotton candy-colored toenails.

His stony eyes gleamed hungrily and the blood in her veins bubbled up to a sizzle. He approached her, one step, then another, eating up the distance in the tiny room until he was close enough for her to make out hunter green specks in the brown of his eyes. She gasped and held her breath.

"You're right. Can't fault a guy for trying to abide by your conditions. You know," he said, fisting the tie of her robe. "No personal contact, unless absolutely necessary."

That had been one of her specifications.

Using the tie, he tugged her forward and swish, personal contact. Just like that. Her body touched his. "Oh."

His knuckles pressed her stomach as he worked his fingers through the loop of the tie. The robe fell open and his heat immediately surrounded her. Like a magnetic force field, she was sucked up, exposed and vulnerable. His eyes drifted down to the negligee underneath the robe. Black lace edging accented sheer peacock blue chiffon.

"What's that called?" He slipped his hands inside the parted robe and caressed her waist.

His fingers stretched out, boldly brushing the top side of her derriere. Her skin prickled and her body shook with slight trembles. There was no way not to react to him, not to enjoy his hands on her, dangerously tempting and delicious.

"B-blue Surrender."

His sharp breath shot to her ears. "Do you always wear your creations to bed?"

She nodded. "Except when I don't."

Jack's mouth cocked up. "You paint a pretty picture, Jillie."

"You asked," she whispered.

"Maybe I shouldn't have." The warmth of his breath fanned her cheeks and she found him inching nearer until his full lips touched her mouth. "Maybe champagne would've been a safer choice," he rasped.

His mouth clamped over hers, claiming her willing lips. Instant shards of hurried heat spiraled down to her belly. She remembered his kiss, the joining of their lips and the way he had of making her feel powerful and beautiful. His lips were rough and firm, taking from her what he wanted too, but also giving. Giving her strength. Giving her pleasure. Giving her what she craved.

He pressed her close, his greedy hands roaming over the sheer fabric of her negligee, searing her body in flames. His fingertips dug in and pressed her with bold and deliberate strokes.

"Oh, Jack," she whispered in a plea.

A tormented groan rose from his throat and he grabbed her upper arms and shoved her back a step, as if keeping her distanced from him would stop his yearning. The kiss with so much promise ended before it really got started. The magical spell was broken.

Jack dropped his hands and stared at her, taking deep breaths. Finally he whispered, "That was absolutely necessary."

Jillian nodded, her gaze trained on his. What could she say to argue the point when the kiss sent her reeling? Everything inside that was dull and tarnished and broken, burst free, bringing polish and luster and shine back to her spirit, if only for the moment.

She found the ties to her robe and crisscrossed them into a knot, then shoved her trembling hands into her pockets to hide them from Jack. Her bravado had failed her. Her first condition of this arrangement, shot to hell.

"Goodnight, Jillian," he said, in his lawman voice.

She listened to his footsteps and then the door shut quietly behind him with a click. She sighed. Lifting her left hand to the fluorescent lighting above, she studied the diamond ring that twinkled with newness and represented more than she'd bargained for.

Whether good or bad, necessary or not, she was getting Jack back.

Temporarily.

THE BELL RANG out overhead in Bluebonnet's Bakery as soon as Jillian stepped one Manolo platform shoe over the threshold. Immediately, she was thrown back in time to her days working here, wearing her cheerful cornflower apron.

Three white wrought iron café tables skirted the perimeter of the shop, the chairs dented and peeling and desperately in need of a makeover. As she stepped further inside the shop, the heel of her shoe caught a chipped linoleum tile and she glanced down at the scratched up flooring. The once whimsical pristine black and white tiles that had always reminded her of Alice in Wonderland were worn to the bone now. Wild bluebonnets, the state flower, stretched across a scenic mural in greeting, yet the birds soaring over blue skies and the wispy blades of grass had faded dully into the wall.

There was nothing cheerful about the place. Nothing noteworthy. Had it only been her youthful exuberance that made her think it so?

She'd been a hard worker, rising early and entering the shop at five in the morning during the summer months to help bake rolls, breads, and toss the doughnuts into big vats. She'd watch the rounded dough float to the surface, puffing up with new life in the bubbling oil. And then as they cooled, she'd frost the doughnuts and then dip them in chocolate sprinkles.

"Coming," said a loud voice from the back room.

Ella Ashton shuffled out in a Bluebonnet's apron, wiping her forehead. Her hair was tucked into a net that matched her brown hair. She was a good twenty pounds heavier than Jillian remembered.

"Hello," Jillian said.

"Hello, what can I get you?" The girl Jillian had gone to school with was peering down at a clipboard as she stopped behind the bakery case.

"I came in to say hello. I'm Jillian Lane. Do you remember me?"

Ella snapped up immediately, her gaze taking a hurried sweep over Jillian, her lips pulling tight. She straightened, as if trying to improve her appearance and pushed away phantom wisps of hair from her brows. "Sure I do. I heard you were back in town."

Ella had never been a fan. She'd had a crush on Jack, like so many other girls. Being the daughter of the owner, she'd made Jillian's work here harder than necessary.

"I'm going to be opening a shop across the street next month. I thought I'd get to know my neighbors again. I'll be having a grand opening. Is your father around? I'd like to say hello to him."

Barney Ashton had always been cordial to her. As a boss, he'd been decent and fair, more than she could say about Ella.

"My dad died three years ago." Ella's voice was emotionless and flat.

Jillian was kicking herself for not doing her homework. She should've asked Jack more questions before heading out today.

"Oh, I'm sorry to hear that. That must be hard on you."

"He left me the bakery. That's my life now. Running this place."

And that was obviously not how Ella had envisioned her future.

"It's not very big, that place across the street. I thought you ran a high-end lingerie store."

She did, but selling lingerie to the folks of Hope Wells didn't warrant a sprawling, all frills shop. And besides, Jillian had always been partial to McGee's Bookstore. She'd spent a good deal of time in there, browsing and buying up copies of the classics from *Jane Eyre* to *The Sun Also Rises*. The old shop meant something to her and she didn't have to think too long or hard about leasing the place while she was still living in Newport Beach. With the economy in a downslide, the bookstore had closed years ago and the owner had given her a good deal on the lease. A little spit and shine on the outside and some renovations inside was all that was needed to complete the transformation. In a sense, opening a shop in Hope Wells was a like a dream come true for Jillian.

"This one will be a Barely There Express."

Ella's brows gathered and she shook her head.

Jillian stifled a chuckle. She'd loved coming up with the concept and a small town like Hope Wells was a perfect place for experimentation. "It's going to be just as grand as my other stores, but on a slightly smaller scale. We'll have inventory and anything not in the store can easily be ordered online."

A light beamed in Ella's eyes for a second before the dullness returned. "Oh."

So sad. Back in high school Jillian would never have guessed she'd feel sorry for Ella. The girl seemed to have a perfect life. "Well, I was hoping to talk to someone about catering desserts for my… uh, engagement party next weekend."

Ella immediately peered over the bakery case, lighting on her diamond ring. "Did you finally snag him? Jack Walker?"

Wow. How was she supposed to answer that? Sometimes, the question spoken told more about the person asking than the answer given. Ella certainly took no prisoners. She'd been uppity then, looking down her nose at Jillian and now she seemed to have somehow perfected that unbecoming quality. It was nothing new, but Jillian's life was different now. She was no longer the poverty-stricken misunderstood girl and obviously, Ella was hardly the prom queen anymore. Her own left hand was bare and yet, she refused to let bygones be bygones.

"Yes, Jack asked me to marry him. And I accepted." That was the truth, without the incendiary details.

"Congratulations." She couldn't have been less enthused. She handed Jillian a brochure. "Here's a list of what we do. Look it over and call the number on the back when you decide what you'd like."

Jillian exited the bakery struck by Ella's attitude. What had happened to Ella Ashton, the popular girl with a mass of friends and great influence in town? It was a pity the girl wasn't living a happier existence. Had she let life drag her down? Had her entitled life somehow turned bitter and cold?

At least Jillian had accomplished one thing today. Ella had always had a gossip grapevine that extended throughout the entire town and surrounding ranches in the area. If that hadn't changed, then by nightfall news of Jack Walker's engagement would spread like wildfire.

She sighed.

The next stop on her agenda this morning was a visit to the *Hope Wells Gazette* where she'd place an engagement announcement. Between the two, by tomorrow everyone in the county would know about her upcoming nuptials.

Chapter Five

Jack exited the hardware store, his arms loaded down with supplies needed to make repairs on his home. Not that the place wasn't livable, but now that he was fake-engaged to Jillian, he had to spruce up the place. A new coat of paint would brighten the drab kitchen walls, a little handiwork to rehinge the bathroom cabinets would keep them from sticking, and installing two new overhead fans would keep the summer heat away. He relished the work that would keep his hands busy. And off Jillian Lane.

Someone bumped his side and a bag of paintbrushes dropped out of his hand. "Ah, damn." He fumbled to keep the rest of his purchases from emptying onto the ground.

"Damn is right, *friend*."

It was Colby and Jack figured the accidental shoulder bump wasn't so accidental. He eyed his high school buddy. "What are to trying to do, knock me to the ground, Cole?"

Colby bent to pick up the paintbrushes. "I should, being as I'm the last to know you got engaged to Jillian." He jammed the bag into Jack's chest. "Had to hear it from one of my hands at the Circle R. What's up with that?"

"Nothin's up. She came back to town and we... reconnected."

"That fast? She's only been in town a few days. Your engagement is already posted in the newspaper from what I hear."

Jack shrugged. Yesterday, Jillian had asked that the announcement be printed as soon as possible and already this morning three people from H.W. Hardware as well as Colby had questioned him about it. By noon, all of Hope Wells would know Sheriff Jack Walker was engaged. Again.

The lies and deception wore on him. All he could do was play the part and hope for the best.

"I mean, I know you always had a thing for her, but when she left town and broke your heart, I thought you'd washed your hands of her."

He had. It had taken him some years, but he'd finally moved on with his life. Yet, there'd been times when he'd catch sight of a blonde woman with a killer body in town from some distance away and his heart would flip, thinking it was Jillian. Or, he'd hear a song on the radio and think of her. Even the sweet smell of strawberries at times, reminded him of how her hair smelled when he kissed her.

"Obviously, things have changed," Jack said. "Jillian came back to open one of her shops in town and... you know how it is."

Colby scrubbed his jaw. "You're sure about this?"

He nodded. There was no doubt his friend was watching

out for him. Jack thought he'd been sure about Jolene, and that had been a disaster. Yet, when she'd left him, he hadn't been all that broken up. It was more embarrassment than heartache that ate at him. He'd let himself believe Jolene was the one for him. And he'd been proven wrong. "I'm sure."

He hated lying to his good friend, but the fewer people who knew about their little marriage bargain, the better. There'd be less chance of the secret getting out and he didn't want to put his friends in the position of having to lie for him. An image of Beau shot into his head reminding him why he was doing this. Yep, he had to stick to the plan.

Colby studied him a moment longer and then stuck out his hand for a shake. "You're forgiven. Congratulations."

They pumped once. "Thanks and sorry for… you know. It's been sort of a whirlwind. We're having an engagement party at the house next Saturday night. You're first on the invitation list."

"Well then, I wouldn't miss it."

And if he was smart, he'd have Dakota on his arm. But Colby was a hard case in that regard.

"Okay then. Talk to you soon, buddy."

They parted in the parking lot and Jack tossed his supplies into the bed of his truck. Instead of heading straight home to start on repairs, he drove down Main Street curious what Jillian was up to. She had her hands full these days, with planning their engagement party and transforming the old bookstore into a high-end lingerie shop. It amazed him how much his life had changed in the one week since he'd found Jillian taking a hot soak at the wells. In a sense she was using him, or as she'd put it, asking him for a favor to get her life and business back on track. But Jack was using her too, to get on the good side of the judge and hope for a favorable outcome with the adoption.

The whole mess left him with a bitter taste in his mouth.

Jillian appeared at the front window inside her shop dressed in jeans, her long hair pulled into a ponytail at the top of her head and the man she was speaking to was eyeballing her like he had the perfect right. Brett Collier. She'd hired him to help with the transformation. It shouldn't unsettle him that Brett was working for her, but the carpenter had an eye for the ladies and right now it seemed Brett was taking aim at Jillian.

Jack parked his truck, a tick working at his jaw. Brett was unmarried, twenty-six years young and spent all of his free time at the gym, building his body and making the single ladies of Hope Wells drool.

As he sauntered into the shop, the quaint door chime rang his presence off tune.

"I'll add that chime to the list or repairs," Brett said, holding Jillian's gaze, the clipboard in his hand forgotten. The guy needed a good strong message and Jack was more than willing to deliver it.

"Hey, sweetheart," Jack said, coming to stand beside Jillian. He wrapped an arm around her waist, splayed his fingers over her hip and drew her up against him.

She stiffened under his palm but plastered a smile on her face, her eyes blinking rapidly and suddenly he'd remembered her number one condition. No touching unless absolutely necessary. Well, hell. This was necessary.

"Hello, Jack."

"Sheriff," Brett said giving him a glance before returning his attention to Jillian.

"What are you doing here?" Her voice carried in the empty room and bounced off walls that still held dusty bookshelves.

"Can't a guy come visit his fiancée just because?" Jack planted a few tiny kisses along Jillian's slender throat and her deep intake of breath made him smile. He was going to pay for that, but it was worth it.

"Oh, yeah, I heard about your engagement," Brett said. "Smart man, taking Miss Lane off the market. Congratulations."

"Thanks," Jack said.

Jillian refused to look at him, turning her attention back to Brett. "Yes, thank you. If there's anything more I can think of, I'll give you a call, Brett."

"Right," he said, tucking his clipboard under his Popeye bicep. "You have my number."

"I'll see you tomorrow then?"

"Sure thing. I'll be here bright and shiny."

As soon as Brett walked outside, Jillian faced him, her

eyes flashing. "What was that all about?"

"What was what all about?"

"You know, Jack Walker."

"I don't know," he said, twisting his lips. Jillian was especially beautiful when she was hot under the collar.

"Why did you kiss me in front of him? Did you want to claim ownership or something?"

"We're supposed let people know we're engaged. Isn't that the plan?"

"I'd already told him we were. And I showed him my engagement ring."

"He probably never saw it, from all the ogling he was doing. The guy couldn't keep his eyeballs in his head."

"Don't tell me you're jealous of Brett?"

"In your dreams." This conversation wasn't going in the right direction.

From the moment he'd walked in here and put a hand on her waist, he'd been overwhelmed with… what? Lust, desire and yeah, jealousy. Which was ridiculous because he wasn't getting seriously involved with Jillian in that way. She was his fake fiancée and they would have a pretend marriage that would last a maximum of twelve months and that was that.

"You are jealous."

"Jillian," he warned. "The guy's a player."

She rolled her eyes. "Trust me, I'm not interested. I've got enough to handle right now." She gave him a pointed look. "And I doubt Brett was ogling. I'm covered in dust, wearing torn jeans and an ancient T-shirt that I should toss in the garbage."

"You do and I'll dig it right out of the trash."

"What?" Puzzled, she shook her head.

"Nothing." There was no point telling her how pretty she looked right now and if he could, he'd take her into his arms and kiss the daylights out of her. Those little pecks he'd given her on the throat had backfired. The more he touched her, the more he wanted to touch her. The more he kissed her, the more he wanted to kiss her. And it wouldn't end there. He wanted to do things to her he'd only imagined in his daydreams. "I like that shirt on you, is all."

He took a few deep breaths and decided Jillian was a three deep breaths kind of girl. She always had been and some things never change. He whipped up a smile. "Is there anything I can do to help you here?"

"No thanks," she said, seeming to recover from their little spat. "I brought my computer. I'm going to do some work online."

"Where?" He looked around the place again.

"There's an old desk in the backroom I can work on."

"Wouldn't you be more comfortable at home?" He meant his guesthouse, but still the words kind of stuck in his throat in a pleasant way that scared the stuffing out of him.

"I think I want to be here and get acclimated. I'll be able to envision the shop and come up with ideas for the floor space."

"Okay, then I'll see you at dinner tonight. I'm grilling."

She looked about ready to decline, but then curiosity lit in her eyes. "You grill?"

"Years of bachelorhood required some degree of cooking on my part. Grilling's my thing, I guess. On my days off that is."

No one would know if they took their meals together or not in the big house Jack owned, but somehow the thought of her being alone in the guesthouse picking at a salad didn't set right with him. Not when he intended to fire up the grill tonight. "You comin'?"

She stared at him, those bright baby blues melt-worthy, doing a number on him as she took her time contemplating. He wished like hell she'd say yes. It wasn't like a date or anything. Shit, how ridiculous that sounded since he was officially engaged to the woman. Even so, he held his breath waiting for her answer.

"Yes, that'd be nice."

He gave her a nod, hiding his relief. "Okay then. I'm off to do some repairs at the house. See you tonight."

He exited the shop, forcing himself not to look back, not to see if her eyes were still on him as he climbed into the cab of his truck. He put the key in the ignition, revved up the engine, and drove off.

Never knowing.

And mentally kicking himself for even wondering.

When the words on the computer screen started blurring together, Jillian knew she'd been at it too long. The dusty backroom that would soon serve as her office and employee lounge was closing in on her. She powered down her computer and rose from the straight back chair to stretch out. Lifting her arms up, she worked at the kinks in her shoulders and rotated her head in winding circles a few times. There. Better.

Where had the time gone? It was already past two in the afternoon and she'd forgotten to eat lunch. Right on cue her stomach began making unfeminine growls and the ridiculous sounds coming from her neglected belly made her smile. Thank goodness, she was alone. Walking from the backroom to the front window of the shop, she glanced outside to witness small-town America in action on a regular weekday. The shops across the street were well kept, the bank to the left solid in red brick, the diner down the street, refurbished with yellow and white tiles and a flashy hand-painted logo on the window. Each shop had a unique quality about them, no two appearing the same. So different than the new trends in big cities, where an entire block's worth of establishments would all sport the same modern design and architecture.

People walked by at an even pace, cars moved slowly down the streets, the open sky above filtered sunshine down until late in the day when the sun would descend the horizon. There were no big buildings or mountains in this ultra flat part of Texas to obstruct the view of the amazing sunsets.

As a girl, Jillian had grown to hate small-town life. She hadn't been treated fairly and it was more small minds rather than the size of the town that had made her wary. In a sense, she was trapped here by circumstances she couldn't control. She was trying to fit in, trying her best to make the time she had here as pleasant as possible.

The corner of the Bluebonnet Bakery brochure stuck out of her purse reminding her she had some things to cross off her list today. Closing up shop, she stood on the sidewalk as two elderly woman approached. She smiled at them, ready to cross the street. To her surprise the women stepped in front of her, and two sets of aged eyes pinned her down, the pinched tight disapproval on their faces almost shocking.

"You're the one opening that X-rated shop right here on Main Street," the taller of the women said.

"Children walk by here," the other said. "It's shameful. All those clothes on display right before their eyes."

Jillian gave her head a quick shake, hardly believing her ears. "I'm sorry?"

"You're not in New York now. This is Hope Wells and we have morals and decency here."

"That's right. You tell her, Marla." The woman speaking was thin and lanky, her back hunched over, as if she couldn't for the life of her straighten up.

She did most of the talking. The other woman was

chunky and wore a colorful dress and an Aunt Bea hat atop her graying hair, making the silent statement that Hope Wells wasn't too far off the mark from Mayberry, USA.

"Ladies, please." She wouldn't bother correcting them that she was from L.A. and not New York. They'd only lump the two together as big city dens of immorality.

"You're connected to that, that, criminal. I read all about it in the newspaper. And to think, you're to marry the finest sheriff in all of Texas." The taller of the two began shaking her head.

Good God. Not this again. Jillian held her tongue when all she wanted was to scream her frustration until her lungs burned. How many times did she have to hear that she wasn't good enough for this town, for the very heroic, highly sought after, Jack Walker?

"Ladies, I can assure you that nothing X-rated will ever be on display in my storefront window. I'm aware of small-town values and, of course, the sensibilities of children, but you might just be surprised at my inventory. Why, I even have lingerie that you both would enjoy. You see, my designs are for all ages… to make a woman feel beautiful. Every woman wants to feel that way. Wouldn't you agree?"

Their brows lifted in unison as if Jillian had actually stunned them. "You should come by when the shop opens and I'll personally find you something soft and silky and warm to wear on cold, lonely nights."

The tall woman gasped. "Well, I never…" But the shorter of the two tilted her head and contemplated.

"And as far as my engagement to Sheriff Walker goes, since he's so highly regarded in this town, clearly his judgment should be considered unequalled. And he chose me."

With that, Jillian stepped off the sidewalk and crossed the street with her head held high as she marched right into the Bluebonnet Bakery.

Once inside, her shoulders slumped against the back of the door, and she was pretty sure it was solely responsible for holding her up. She sighed from deep in her chest and allowed her gaze to skitter across the room to the bakery counter where Ella was holding back a smirk. Crapola. Not her, too. She turned around to let herself out. She wasn't up for another round of Miss Grumpy Pants giving her grief, but before her hand turned the doorknob, Ella spoke up.

"Those two old biddies giving you trouble?"

She turned to face Ella. Jillian had enough on her plate right now, but in that moment she decided she wasn't going to give Ella or the two elderly ladies the satisfaction of knowing they'd gotten to her. "I can handle them."

"They're the Barker cousins and I wouldn't let them get you down. They don't approve of anything that isn't puritanical in this town. They tried to stop prom night at the high school once and when that didn't go over well, they moved onto protesting the movie theatre for showing R-rated movies."

"Well, I appreciate you telling me that."

"They're harmless and from what I could tell, you told them off pretty darn good."

"But I didn't." She walked further into the bakery. "I simply told them the truth. My designs are for young and old alike. Barely There, sure it sounds sexy and some of my designs certainly are, but it's all about being comfortable and stylish in your own skin. That's the *barely there* I was getting at when I started my business. I wanted to design apparel that is so sleek and smooth and comfy that you barely know you're wearing it."

"Really?"

"Yeah, really. That was my intent and I try to hold true to that, no matter if it's a pair of see-through baby dolls or a long nightgown. All my stuff is ultra comfortable."

Ella blinked and cleared her throat as if a frog had taken up residence in there. "I see. Uh, what can I get you?"

"A cup of coffee please, black is fine and a bagel or something. I haven't eaten since breakfast. If you have a minute, maybe you can sit down with me and we can go over the list of bakery items I'd like to order for my engagement party."

Ella's big amber eyes rounded and for a minute Jillian saw the girl she'd once been. When those eyes landed on a boy with a flirty smile, the guy was history. Jillian couldn't imagine the weight of all that pressure, being the class favorite, having girls emulate her, having a string of boys at your beck and call. Ella's life hadn't measured up to those high school glory days and that must be a crushing blow to her. "Oh, I guess I can take a minute. It's not too busy right now."

It wasn't busy at all. Ella's bakery didn't seem to be doing well through the bad economy. She had competition. The grocery stores had their own bakeries filled with breads, bagels, and doughnuts. But it was more than that. Ella didn't enjoy the work. It was apparent by her attitude and by the way she'd let the place go.

She brought over two cups of coffee and an *everything* bagel loaded with cream cheese. They sat down at a café table. "Thanks again," Jillian said, "for making me feel better about those Barker women."

Ella shrugged. "I wouldn't worry about them."

She smiled, taking a big bite of her bagel. Her stomach rejoiced. "I won't. I've had enough opposition coming back here."

Ella regarded her, tilting her head. "I suppose it's only natural. You're big news in town. People seem to like a scandal."

"How well I know. But I had no part in all that illegal stuff. I've been cleared of all charges. I'm hoping to put that behind me now."

"It's not always easy." Ella's voice faltered and sadness swept over her expression.

Jillian stared, surprised by her comment and the way Ella suddenly directed her gaze to the tabletop. Jillian couldn't let that comment go. "Are you speaking from experience?"

"Haven't you heard?"

Jillian gave her head a shake. "Heard what?"

Ella's lips sealed tight.

"You don't have to tell me if it's too painful," Jillian said after a time.

She was dying to know, but she was never one to pry. She took a sip of coffee.

"I haven't spoken about it for quite some time, but…" Ella paused as if deciding whether to open up to her. "I suppose we're in the same boat now. Kind of." She sighed. "The short version is that I came home on spring break during my junior year in college and got engaged to Paul McKenzie. We were so much in love and looking forward to our wedding after I graduated college."

Paul McKenzie was born into one of the wealthiest families in Texas, ranching and oil made for a huge family empire. Jillian had never cared for the guy. She'd refused him flat about a dozen times after he'd made it known he wanted a one night hookup with her rather than a real date. After he tired of her refusals, he'd spread vicious rumors about her at school. And Jack had nearly busted Paul's nose when he found out what he'd been saying.

Ella smiled sheepishly. "I know now that Paul wasn't loyal to me. He didn't really love me."

"What happened?"

"To put it bluntly, one night we walked in on my father and Paul's mother going at it. They were buck naked in some twisty position in the McKenzie wine cellar. I'll spare you the details, but Paul blamed my father for everything. He said some pretty horrendous things, which in that moment I understood. We were both shocked, but Paul wouldn't let it go. He told his father immediately what we'd discovered and then went straight to my mother. When the news broke in the community, I think it was hardest on my mom. Paul and I split up. We just couldn't seem to look at each other in the same way. And my mom tried to... well, months later, she swallowed half a bottle of sleeping pills. Luckily, she survived it all, but that and divorcing my father left her extremely fragile."

"And so you're here, trying to keep the bakery going to support her?"

"Yeah, there were some dark days back then and the bakery was the one constant I had in my life."

"But you don't like it much."

She shook her head. "I enjoy creating and making pastries, testing new recipes, but not the rest. Making doughnuts and bread every day bores me to death." She took a sip of coffee. "So now you know."

Ella put her head down to go over the order Jillian had handed her.

"I know one thing, you and I aren't very different at all," she said softly.

"Maybe not," Ella whispered.

"Ella," Jillian said, pulling the order list out of her hand

and getting her attention. "Why don't you make us eight dozen of your finest pastries? Create something wonderful, something you enjoy making. And then please, stay for the party."

Ella's eyes lit for a moment and then she glanced away, blinking. "I don't want your pity."

"It's not pity, Ella. We're old friends. We've both been through hard times lately. Come, and enjoy a night out. It would mean a lot to me."

"Why? I was never nice to you in school."

"We're not in school anymore, are we?"

Ella chuckled and glanced at the bakery as if it were her prison. "Hardly."

"Just say you'll think about it."

"I can do that." And then Ella smiled.

JILLIAN WALKED THROUGH Jack's backyard gate, lured by the smoky scents rising up from the grill. The size of a man's grill told its own story and Jack's two-burner, rotisserie enabled barbeque grill had serious written all over it. He wasn't anywhere in sight, but a spice rubbed brisket and sliced veggies were coaxing her forward. "Jack?"

"In here," he called from inside the house and as she followed the sound of his voice, she found him in the parlor, high atop a ladder, fidgeting with the blades of a new fan.

"Watch your step."

His warning came just in time and she sidestepped a mess of old fan parts on the floor. The view though, from where she stood made her mouth go dry.

"Almost done," he said, using a screwdriver.

"Take your time." She shouldn't look at his ass, but he'd never know and he had a fine one, perfect in a pair of washed-out jeans, slung ultra-low on his hips. His shirt was off too, making him naked from the waist up. That word, *naked*. It did things to her when describing Jack Walker and her heartbeats sped. She inhaled from deep in her lungs to replace the oxygen that just pushed out in a gasp.

"What'd you say?" he asked, focused on that last blade.

"Uh, I brought dessert."

"Oh, yeah?"

She was staring at her dessert, up there, shirtless, guileless, so intent on his task. He was breaking another of her conditions. *Keep our clothes on, around each other.* It had been in the interest of keeping things from getting hot and heavy, but had she really demanded that of him? Apparently, she couldn't tell a man what he could and could not wear in his own home. Well, she could and did, but he hadn't listened.

"Lawman food."

He finally glanced down at her. "What in hell is lawman food?"

"Doughnuts from the bakery."

"That's not lawman food. Unless of course, you brought

me a maple bar." He turned on the ladder and gave her a hopeful look. Seeing all that muscle and bare flesh could give a girl hives.

She opened the bakery box and showed him half a dozen.

"Oh man, Jillian," he said nearly drooling, and giving her a glimpse of what it would be like if Jack ever craved her, the same way he did his favorite doughnut.

He climbed down, finished with the installation of the fan. "I'm tempted," he said gazing at the box.

"Go for it, Jack." She moved the box closer to him. It was the only thing separating her from his almost naked body. "Dessert first. It's not against the law."

He laughed and all of those chest muscles rippled.

She stuffed the end of a maple bar into her mouth. "See," she said, chewing, "it can be done."

He reached for his white T-shirt and pulled it over his head, concealing mouthwatering abs. It was daunting, watching him *put on* his clothes—seeing soft cotton caress his skin until it settled at the waistband of his jeans—making her heart pound hard.

What had come over her? Was it the kiss the night of their deceptive engagement? Was it simply seeing him nearly naked? Was it something more, something unnamed?

She wasn't going to do this with Jack. She couldn't risk taking advantage of him again, or hurting his chances with the adoption. She had to keep her head together. They had made a mutual pact to help each other. Getting involved again would cause damage in the end. Hadn't the entire town told her that, umpteen times? But the town hadn't told her anything she didn't already believe. She wasn't good for Jack Walker. So, she had to cool the lust going on inside her head.

For Jack.

For Beau.

For her own sanity.

On her dare, he reached in and grabbed a doughnut and stuffed half of it into his mouth, his dark eyes glittering.

"You're a daredevil, Sheriff Walker."

"Maybe you bring that out in me."

"Maybe, I shouldn't."

He dug his teeth into the other half of the doughnut. "You can't help it, Jillian."

No, no she couldn't. She watched him enjoy the maple bar with gusto and then walked into the kitchen. "One's all you're getting before dinner."

He followed her. "Yes, because we don't want to be too wild and crazy."

"Yeah, having two or three, now that would break the lawman code or something, right?" She set her half eaten doughnut on a napkin.

"Absolutely." He went to the sink and ducked under, splashing water on his face and then washing his hands. Drying off with a towel, he asked, "Want a soda or beer?"

"Just water, thanks. I'll get it."

He took a glass from the cabinet and handed it to her. She moved to the front of the refrigerator and pressed the ice button and then filled her glass. Jack's eyes were on her as she moved about his kitchen.

"Are you hungry?" he asked, grabbing a beer for himself.

"Not really. Not after downing half of that doughnut."

"Me either." He shrugged. "Guess there are some consequences when we don't play by the rules."

She got the feeling he wasn't talking about dessert first anymore.

"I'll go shut down the grill for now. We'll eat a little later."

She followed him outside. After he did his grill master thing with the food, he gestured for her to take a seat on the brick patio. She chose a padded lawn chair that faced a well-groomed garden and Jack leaned against a thick beam that held up the patio cover. The house was spacious and the lawn was equally large, green grass that met his neighbor's green grass without benefit of fencing. She had always wondered at the borderless properties, even though she'd grown up in Texas. Where she'd lived, a tiny shack compared to Jack's place, the houses had been stacked close together and rusted chain link fences divided the backyards. In Newport, her home now, and in L.A, where she worked, property lines were often in dispute causing major upheavals and lawsuits so the openness here was refreshing to her. "What do people do if they have dogs?"

Jack laughed again. It was as if the question wasn't what he expected. "They put up hedges. Fences aren't out of the question either. I have a fence out front."

"That's decorative. It's not really functional."

"True enough."

"What about kids? What will you do if you get Beau?"

Jack's brow furrowed, taking the question seriously now. "I suppose, I can fence in around the patio area, until he gets older."

"So you've given this some thought."

"I have. I don't claim to know all there is about parenting…"

"You'll be a great dad, Jack. I have no doubt."

"If I'm able to adopt Beau." His mouth curved down just enough for her to see his worry. Then he sipped his beer.

"I'll do whatever I can to help make that happen."

He gestured with the beer bottle in one hand making a wide arc. "That's why we're doing all this. I hope it's enough."

All this, meaning lying to everyone about their engagement and marriage. "Me too."

"I got some things done today to make the house more livable. Fixed shutters, put up two new fans. I intend to paint a few rooms too, before we have the engagement party."

"I'll help."

"Thanks, but you've got your hands full with opening

your shop. I'll manage." He sipped beer again, downing the rest of the bottle. And though refusing her help seemed to fit his manly man nature, as well as giving her time to work on her own things, she halfway suspected Jack was avoiding having to work alongside her for any reason. He didn't want her here. Period. Her showing up in Hope Wells had ruined his plans.

"I guess…" He scratched his head, and the words he wanted to form seemed to die on his lips.

"You guess what?" She leaned forward a bit, wondering why he looked like he'd just bitten into a rotten egg. His face contorted, his generous mouth looking impossibly grim.

"We, uh, also need to plan the wedding. Should happen soon."

Yes, she supposed it should. But once again, the very idea of marrying her seemed to be like poison to Jack's system. She tried not to be hurt by the look on his face, the tone of his voice. But it did hurt and she couldn't deny it.

"How soon?"

He got this blank look on his face. "However long it takes to plan one of these things."

She didn't really know. She'd never planned a wedding before, parties yes, weddings no.

"Okay."

"The smaller the ceremony the better," he said. "I mean, we're having this splashy engagement party and all. The wedding doesn't have to be—"

"I get it, Jack. You want a small ceremony. Perhaps just

with family and close friends?"

"Maddie said she'd help and offered up 2 Hope Ranch for the nuptials. It's pretty there." He scratched his head, clearly uncomfortable with the subject. "Unless it's not what you want."

What exactly did she want? The details were beginning to cloud up. Seeing her soon-to-be husband on that ladder, abs beautifully exposed, messed with her head a little. She had the hots for Jack Walker, just like always. And, just like always, he was pushing her away.

Yet, she was going to be Jack's bride and at least he cared enough to ask about her wedding day desires. The truth was, though, her brain was telling her not to make a big deal out of it, yet this was to be her first ever wedding. A girl always dreamed of her wedding day, what her dress would look like, speaking her vows, and mostly about the man that would stand by her side and make promises to her, about their future.

"Jillian?"

She'd been caught daydreaming. How very dumb of her. This was not real. None of it was and putting Jack's gorgeous near nakedness aside, she had to remember that. "It's very nice of her. I think we should do it."

"Okay, I guess the next step is to take you to the ranch and introduce you to Maddie. I think you remember my cousin, Trey."

"I sure do." She nodded. "I'd like that."

"There's just one thing they both don't know…"

Chapter Six

THE NEXT EVENING, a blazing tangerine sun was beginning to lower on the horizon as Jack and Jillian walked up to greet Maddie Walker on the steps of her home at 2 Hope Ranch. Jack quickly made introductions and it was clear by his tone more than any one particular thing, that Jack thought the world of his cousin's wife. Often, his deep voice would give way to a softer pitch whenever her name came up in conversation.

"It's nice to meet you, Jillian," Maddie said. "Congratulations on your engagement and upcoming marriage. Trey and I are very excited for both of you."

"Thank you," Jillian said. "It all seems to be happening so fast." Which was the truth, but there were too many lies behind it to make Jillian feel good about any of this.

In a sign of affection, Maddie put a hand on Jack's upper arm. "Sometimes it doesn't take long to know when it's right."

Maddie was adorably pregnant. She wore a belly bump exceedingly well under a plaid shirt and jeans that were probably unbuttoned at the waistband. Trey's wife was gracious enough not to pry into Jillian and Jack's quick engagement, making her rare and kind in Jillian's eyes. Since Jack hadn't told his cousin and his wife the exact terms of this hasty marriage, a fact that Jillian wasn't sure she understood, the obvious gossip floating around Hope Wells had to be that Jack had knocked Jillian up. At least that was what immediate engagements and quickie marriages had meant when Jillian was growing up here. But, as far as she knew, those marriages hadn't come with a time limit. Like Jillian's would. She'd agreed to Jack's terms without really thinking it through, but now she was too deep to have second thoughts. And young Beau Riley's future was at stake.

An awkward moment passed.

Jack, the traitor, had his mouth clamped shut and forced a smile, leaving it up to Jillian to respond. What choice did she have but to agree? And really, what was one more lie in a sea of deception? "Yes, that's absolutely true. When it's right, you know it."

She glanced into Jack's eyes and saw a flicker, a raw emotion escaping in his silence that he immediately tried to conceal. She gave her attention back to Maddie and changed the subject. "I understand you've got some excitement coming soon too. Congratulations. When is the baby due?"

Maddie laid a hand on her belly, an age-old gesture that touched Jillian's heart every time an expectant mother did that. As if to say, *I don't even know my sweet baby yet, but I'd go to the ends of the earth to protect it.*

"I'm not due for awhile yet. I'm four months along but, honestly, the time seems to be flying by. Trey and I can hardly believe that he or she will be here before we know it." And then Maddie gestured to the door. "Please come in. Trey's just getting cleaned up."

They entered the house and no sooner had they walked into the parlor, Trey strode into the room smelling like lime soap and looking healthy and tall and handsome, his dark hair curling at his shoulders, a little damp at the ends. He wasn't as broad in the shoulders as Jack, he never had been, but his features were as sharp and defined. There was definitely a family resemblance. Walker men were not hard on the eyes.

"Jillian Lane, get on over here," Trey said, not giving her a chance to move. His strides were long and swift and before she knew it she was on the receiving end of a giant hug. She hugged him back and the strength and welcome of his arms felt good.

"Trey, it's good to see you."

"Same here," he said, stepping back to meet her eyes. His were twinkling. "You sure you know what you're doing, marrying my cousin. I always thought you were smarter than that."

Jack's smile twisted sideways. "Hey."

She laughed. The two were close, like brothers and had always given each other grief. Jillian remembered Trey Walker being less friendly, less happy back in high school though, but Jack told her Maddie had changed all that. Actually, he'd said, she'd rocked his world.

"Congrats on the baby, Trey. I'm happy for you."

He put an arm around his wife and she settled in next to him, hip to hip, their contact so easy, Maddie looking at Trey like the sun set on his shoulders. Jillian felt a pang of envy. Their happiness was evident of their faces, in the solid way Trey held his wife, in the way they seemed to be of one mind, one heart. How lovely and unique. That baby was one lucky child.

"Thanks, we're pretty happy about it too."

"We've got a few minutes of daylight left," Maddie said, "if you'd like to look over the grounds and find the perfect place for the wedding to take place. I'll put dinner on hold."

Jillian glanced at Jack and he nodded.

"That would be nice," she said.

Trey and Maddie gave them the grand tour of the house, the backyard, the corral area, the barns and the path leading to Maddie's gardens. Aside from being a veterinarian, she dabbled in raising flowers. Gorgeous yellow mums and pink lilies bloomed across the lawn. "They're lovely," Jillian said.

"I started the garden after we got married. Trey and I spoke our vows right over there, on horseback," Maddie said pointing to an arbor of lush vines. "It's a special place for us and if you'd like to have the ceremony there, we wouldn't mind at all."

"It's gonna be small affair," Jack said.

"But meaningful," Maddie insisted. "And it's the bride's choice."

"It's beautiful here," Jillian said, gazing out beyond the lawn to where the sun was beginning to descend. "I think so. I think just about this time of day too."

"The sunsets here are pretty kickass," Trey stated.

Jack snorted and gave his cousin a smirk. "Trey's got a way with words."

"You're an ass," Trey countered but with a wide smile on his face.

"I've been called much worse."

"Yeah, by me."

Jack had always been the more vocal of the two, the charmer, the man who never let a mishap or verbal mistake go without a teasing jab. That hadn't changed.

"Are you two through yet?" Maddie piped in, shaking her head and turning to speak solely to Jillian now. "Most times, I'm the only grown-up in the room. I'm glad I'll have you now, another reasonable female in the family to help keep the sanity."

Jillian darted a look at Jack. His eyes had rounded as if… as if he just now realized that Maddie too, could get hurt when their temporary arrangement ended. Oh, boy. None of this was going to be easy.

"I'll do my best, Maddie. But boys will be boys."

"Ain't that the truth."

"So, when is all this happiness gonna happen?" Trey

asked. "Do you have a date for the wedding?"

Jillian pulled her upper lip in and began nibbling. She turned to Jack, tossing him the ball so to speak.

He stepped up. "I figure in three weeks. We're doing a splashy engagement party next weekend, so the wedding will be—"

"I know, a small affair," Trey finished for him.

"Only, if that works for you, Maddie? It's kinda quick and asking a lot of you." There was no mistaking Jack's gratitude or the humble tone he was taking.

She nodded. "It works. Just give me the guest list and I'll do the rest."

"Because you don't have enough to do, with the animals, the flowers, the baby, and taking care of this guy over here," Jack said.

"I consider it an honor to help plan your wedding," Maddie countered. "So, it's settled then? We'll have the ceremony here in three weeks."

Jillian liked Maddie's decisive nature. She was a doer and Jillian had surrounded herself with people, women mostly, who knew how to get a job done. She wasn't patting herself on the back but she was proud of the company she'd developed. Darn proud and if it wasn't for her involvement with Enrique Vasquez, her company would still be making great strides.

"Thank you," Jillian said. "Please remember, I'm available to help with anything and everything."

"We'll make it work, don't you worry," Trey said, giving her a nod.

And, suddenly, just like that, Jillian's stomach began to ache. She was in over her head again and there seemed to be no way out and these people, these wonderful, generous people who were willing to go great lengths for Jack, for *family*, reminded her once again how truly shallow and sad, her own family had been. It hurt her on some level but it also was testament to the basic good in people. In Jack. And the Walkers.

"Thanks, man." Jack said, in a gravelly voice as he gave Trey's shoulder a squeeze. That small gesture, steeped in deep love and affection was over in a second, but the impact gripped her hard and a tear threatened to drip from her eye. She turned her head and swiped at it before anyone noticed her wrapped so heavily in emotion.

One would think she was the pregnant one, going all hormonal like this, holding back tears and wishing she'd never returned to Hope Wells in the first place.

DURING DINNER MADDIE and Jillian discussed several details of the wedding. It was truly going to be casual and simple with no more than twenty friends and family in attendance. That suited Jillian just fine. The less fuss, the less guilt. Jack felt the same way, although, after seeing Maddie's enthusiasm in arranging all of this, their guilt factor would probably have to be recalculated.

The wedding meal would be served inside the house and there would be music out on the back lawn, where they would also serve the cake. With input from Jillian and because time was short, Maddie was going to design and send out invitations by email. Maddie offered to take Jillian shopping for just the right wedding dress. She could hardly refuse the kind offer, although what Jillian had in mind to wear was more of a wedding suit, than a long flowing gown.

As they finished the meal, Jack took a look at the fatigue on Maddie's face and immediately rose from his seat. He reached for Jillian's hand and helped her up too. The contact surprised her, and warmth seeped into her bones as Jack's hand closed over hers. "Time to let the baby mama get some sleep."

"I agree," Jillian said. "We should let you get to bed. Maddie, Trey, I can't thank you enough for everything you're doing for us."

"You're welcome," Maddie said. "It will be fun making it all come together."

"What she said," Trey added. "Happy to do it."

"Can I help with the dishes?" Jillian asked, realizing the table wasn't cleared yet.

"Nope," Trey said. "I've got that covered. Won't take but a minute to do cleanup."

"I think that's our cue to leave," Jack said, grinning, and

tugged her toward the front door.

Trey and Maddie said goodnight from the front porch. Jillian figured it had to be the reason Jack unlocked their fingers and put his hand to the small of her back. As he guided her along, she absorbed his touch, the possessive way his hand held her firm as they walked the path leading toward his car. Having him touch her did crazy things to her body. Jolts and sparks and tingles, she felt it all when he put his hands on her. It was just for show and she was silly to think much of it, but as he opened the car door and she slid into her seat, her dress rode up her thighs and his eyes grazed her legs with enough heat to set her on fire.

Oh, boy.

And after he climbed into the driver's seat and started the engine, she caught him taking another peek of her legs before clearing his throat and driving off.

If they ever did get together, they'd combust. For sure.

"They're nice," she said to Jack after a minute of silence. "Trey's head over heels for Maddie. I can tell by the way he looks at her," she said.

Jack nodded.

"What they have together is very special. Not everyone gets that lucky."

Jack bobbed his head in agreement.

"They clearly love you very much to be willing to plan the whole wedding."

Jack grunted something unintelligible.

Okay, so he wasn't in the mood for small talk and she didn't want to sit in silence on the way home, not when she had a lot on her plate. She dug into her purse and plucked out her cell phone. It was two hours earlier on the west coast and surely early enough not to wake anyone up. "Mind if I make a call while we're driving back?"

"It's your dime," he said, keeping his eyes on the road.

Jillian dialed her office manager's number and she picked up on the first ring. "Hey, Jillian. How's it going deep down in the heart of Texas?"

God, it was good to hear Tessa's voice. In the years since she'd opened Barely There, her office manager had become much more. They were best friends now and Tess was someone Jillian trusted in her life. After the fiasco with Enrique, trust wasn't easy to come by so Tessa's friendship was important to her. "It's going. I'm on schedule for the grand opening right after I get married."

Tessa chuckled. "Good one, Jillian."

"I'm serious. I'm getting married in a few weeks and wanted to personally invite you to the wedding." Out of the corner of her eye, she saw Jack flinch, but he kept his eyes on the road. Maybe speaking to Tessa now wasn't such a great idea.

"Is it the hot sheriff you told me about?" Thank God Tessa wasn't on speakerphone.

"Uh, yeah."

"You're really doing this?"

"Uh, yeah. I'll explain later, I promise."

"So this is my save the date, phone call?"

"You got it," Jillian said. "I hope you can come."

"I wouldn't miss it, Jill. I'll be there, just text me the details."

"I'll do that. So, how's it going in L.A? Anything happening that I should know about?"

"Well, uh. It's nothing really, but our office building was egged the other night. Found evidence of it all over the door and windows."

"Really?"

"Yeah, but it wasn't anything serious. We had it cleaned up right away. And everything's been quiet since then. Sales are down across the board, but that could be for a whole slew of reasons."

More like, her business being associated with a drug operation. "We'll get it back once everything dies down."

She'd taken a big risk coming back to Hope Wells to start up a new branch of her company, when the last two quarterly sales had taken an immense drop. But she wasn't one to quit and she was determined to ride out this storm. The egg thing at her head office had to be a prank of some sort, a group of teens, an irrational customer who got his jollies in some weird way, but that too, would pass. Jillian was all-in when she wanted something and she wanted Barely There to survive. It was just about all she had in life lately.

After the conversation ended, she texted Tessa the wedding details and tossed her phone back into her purse. "She's my best friend," she explained, just in case Jack wanted to talk. "I really want her to be at the wedding."

Apparently, Jack didn't have anything to add to the one-sided conversation, so Jillian remained quiet during the rest of the drive home. There was something eating at him and her curiosity was not to be stilled regardless that it had killed the cat. It might kill her too, because she ached inside seeing the way Jack was acting right now. Had it finally hit him? Had making the plans for their marriage scared him to death? Because he was not alone in that. Getting married had been solely his idea. Jillian had had her bags packed, literally, and was willing to walk away, but he'd called her back and come up with the idea of marriage.

He pulled the car into the driveway and she got out before he could come around and open the door. He stood by the hood of his car now, watching her through lowered lids.

She couldn't keep quiet another second. "What is it Jack? Why the silent treatment?"

He clenched his jaw and set his chin onto an invisible layer of air as if it was a shelf. Oh, God. He was going to be stubborn. "Nothin'."

"Something." She walked over to him, looking him dead in the eye. "Tell me."

He kept his mouth clamped.

"I need to know what's going on in your head." She persisted, staring into his eyes.

He stared back for beats of a minute, and then his rigid shoulder gave way, an inch, maybe less, but it was enough of a crack in his armor.

She pressed him again. "Please, tell me."

His face unmasked and he sighed. "Not here."

"Where?"

He grabbed her hand and tugged her toward his house. They entered, her following behind him, the heat of his grasp sending sizzling jolts through her body. As soon as the door closed behind them, Jack backed her up against the wall, his big frame nearly swallowing her up. Once she got over the initial shock of his uncharacteristic move, she lifted her lids to find a dark gleam of hunger in his eyes. Moonlight filled the room in a soulful illumination that matched what she was feeling inside. A ray, a shock of hope and desire? Jack was looking at her the way he had back when they were in love, like he wanted to devour her and lap at every ounce of her flesh with his tongue.

The memory of their heated kisses that would go nowhere but a cold shower for him and disappointment for her, filled her mind. She wasn't immune to him, she never had been. She was the risk taker usually and her brain wanted to hear what he had to say, while her body was aching for his touch. "What is it?" she whispered, hearing the desperation in her voice.

"I don't like breaking rules," he said.

Of course not, he was the law.

"But I'm gonna break them with you."

And then his fingertip touched her cheek so exquisitely that her breath caught in her throat. Oh, God. The way he was looking at her. He trained his eyes directly on her and only her as if he'd blocked out everything else. He ran his finger to just below her mouth and circled the outline of her lips. Over and under, over and under.

She began to quake inside. "Y-you are?"

"Uh huh," he said, his eyes focused, very focused on the lips she just parted. "I can't not touch you, honey. And I can't guarantee you're not gonna see me naked, or that I'm not gonna see you naked. It's necessary..."

A shudder rippled through her body just as he dipped his head and put his mouth on hers. It was hot and delicious and so very *necessary*. He smelled of lime aftershave, bright and fresh and clean. He was a hero, no matter how many times he denied it. He was honest and true and selfless, but he was sexy as hell too, especially now as she tasted from his smooth, calculating, tempting lips.

He pressed closer to her trapped body and a whimper escaped her throat as the feel of his hard shaft meshed against her belly. Oh, wow. Her heart hammered fiercely, his arousal unleashing her own dormant desires. Awakened now, and so in tune with him, her nerves jumped for joy against her skin. Every brain cell that normally clicked in overtime, shut down completely. As he kissed her thoroughly, mating their tongues, she wrapped her arms around his neck, pulling him closer and earning from him a guttural groan of approval.

Tension sizzled in the air; their kisses grew hotter, heavier, going long and deep, tantalizing every single inch of her body. And just as she was thinking it, feeling it, down to her very soul, Jack backed away, his mouth no longer on hers and the loss of his departure was sharp and keen.

He touched their foreheads and took several long steadying breaths. "Babe, I'm not sure this is gonna work."

It was working just fine a few seconds ago. "Why not?" she asked, breathless.

"You're gonna be moving into this house soon. Should probably already be living here." He rasped. "And those rules of yours…"

As if to prove his point, he set his hands on the sides of her torso and the pads of his thumbs grazed over her breasts. Even through the material of her dress, the heat and pressure surged her nipples to a rosy rounded point. She shuddered visibly and moaned. "Jack." His name came out as a plea.

"I can't abide by your conditions, Jillian. I thought I could, but it's too hard. It's too much to ask of me, when all I want to do whenever I see you, is…"

She lifted her lids to give him her full attention. "Is what, Jack?" she whispered.

"You want me to say it?"

His hands cupped her breasts now and the ache in her belly drifted further south. "Yes. Say it." She pleaded, loving the feel of his palms flattened on her chest.

"I want to be inside you, baby. I want to make love to you all night long. It would be so fucking good between us."

Images immediately raced to her mind, of Jack doing that very thing to her. Of her lying with him, giving herself up to him. Being *inside* her. Oh, yeah. She'd dreamt of it, fantasized about it and now Jack had finally admitted how much he wanted her. In this moment, anyway.

"I like it when you talk dirty, Jack."

His head jerked back and his eyes rounded. "Shit, Jillian." He couldn't seem to hold back laughter. "You are too much."

She batted her eyes. "I am. Let me show you."

Another groan erupted from his throat and then his arms were under her knees and she was being lifted and carried effortlessly by this big, strong man toward his bedroom.

JACK DIDN'T CARE that he was breaking rules all over the place, the conditions Jillian had set up when they'd agree to this ruse, tossed out like yesterday's trash. He wasn't going to feel bad about this. About her. She'd been a torment on his brain since the moment he'd met her all those years ago and he was through trying to keep things sane and rational. Maybe what he needed right now was a little insanity. A little wild and crazy. He could do wild and crazy, in the bedroom.

Sure. With Jillian, he got the feeling all things were possible on that score.

As he stepped into his bedroom, her clinging to his neck, her sweetly sensual scent filling his nostrils, his rock hard body grew even harder. How was that even possible? It must have something to do with the beautiful woman hanging onto him, bestowing mind-blowing kisses onto his throat, her long blonde hair tickling his chin. Holy crap. How was a man supposed to think straight?

He lowered her down until her feet hit the floor. He wanted her on the bed, but not just yet. Not until he peeled off her clothes. Not until she stood before him stark naked, a blank canvas that he would paint tonight with his hands, his mouth, his cock.

Hell, she wanted it wild and dirty. He could accommodate.

Jillian wasn't the only one who could do shock and awe.

Her arms still clung to his neck and he unfolded her, taking her hands in his and bringing his mouth to hers in a quick firm kiss. Then he let her go and walked behind her. His lips caressed her shoulder blades at her back, first one then the other, and his fingers found the zipper of her dress. Slowly, the teeth of the zipper pulled apart to expose the creamy softness of her back and the sexy pink lace bra that housed two perfect breasts. Jack unhooked the fastener and scooped his hands inside to cup the soft globes. He gave them a little squeeze.

Her breath hitched.

His cock surged.

God, Jillian was killing him. And he hadn't even gotten her dress off yet. "I would dream about doing this to you," he said, not worried about admitting this to her.

"So would I," she confessed.

Jack smiled and spread his hands wide, allowing the dress and bra to fall to the floor, bunching around Jillian's high heeled shoes. Everything she wore tonight was pink, including a pair of panties that wasn't quite a thong. The lace that touched her cheeks dipped down to a vee into her crease. He spun her around then, anxious to see the front view. He wasn't disappointed. The lace was sheer at the apex of her thighs, barely hiding the tiny layer of curls that were sculpted and shaped into a heart. Good God.

He almost hated removing them, they were that hot, but then he reminded himself of the blank canvas of his dreams and off they went, his finger hooking the thin waistband and lowering them down all the way to her toes. She gave them a little kick and they vanished from sight.

"You blow me away, Jillian," he murmured.

"And you have too many clothes on, Jack."

He shook his head. "Not yet, babe. We're not rushing this." He wanted to gaze at her, memorize her, drink her in. She was tall and blonde and beautiful, with intelligent eyes that sparkled like blue gems and hair that cascaded in waves of gold.

Blood pulsed through his veins as he moved closer and finally touched her, on the shoulders, framing her beautiful form, and then slowly he moved his hands down her torso, grazing the outer edge of her breasts, the nipples he'd touched before, instantly forming twin, tight lovely pink buds.

He took a gulp of air. Pressure built in his groin. It was a bit of torture for him and maybe for her too, but he needed to do this, wanted it so badly and didn't have the willpower to stop on his own accord. Luckily for him, Jillian wasn't stopping him either and she appeared as turned on as he was.

His hands found her waist, the indent that shaped her female body and then went lower still, to where the beauty of that heart shape met with the soft folds of her skin. He trailed his finger along that path and touched her entrance.

She swallowed a cry and when he slid his finger across the delicate sensitive folds, he met with moisture. She was wet for him. Goddamn. "You don't know what it does to me, to have you like this."

He slammed his mouth over hers and took her in a hot heady kiss. She tasted slightly of chablis and he licked at her lips once, twice, and then got busy stroking her, one hand cupping her ass, holding her steady as the fingers of his other hand tantalized and teased her folds.

She started making gasping noises, but he wasn't through exploring her body. He had so much more to do and he dropped to his knees, gripped her ass in both hands now and kissed those heart-shaped curls until he was nearly drunk on the taste of her.

She moved and rocked her body, swaying and jutting her hips. He didn't let up, the tension mounting and her gasps of pleasure coming quicker now, louder.

"I'm so close, Jack." She gritted out. "I'm, ah—" Her voice elevated and her gasps turned to unrelenting moans.

Seeing her passionate, vulnerable, and at the peak of pleasure was the sexiest thing Jack had ever witnessed. Her hands were in his hair now, tugging, holding him in place, as she gave in to the sensations, surrendering to the climax taking control now.

Her sounds vibrated in his ears and turned him inside out.

"Jack, oh, Jack."

"I'm here, babe," he said as she finished. Then he rose to give her a kiss and take her into his arms. She was soft and pliant, limp against him. "You okay?"

She sighed. "I'm better than okay." And after a minute, she whispered, "And you still have too many clothes on."

Even though he was aching with the hardest hard-on, a chuckle pushed out of his mouth. Then he got down to business, unsnapping his shirt, kicking off his boots and Jillian was right there with him, pushing his arms out of his sleeves and unbuckling his belt. Once he was naked, a fleeting thought of the rules that they were breaking flashed, for half a second, before he discarded them and backed

Jillian to the edge of the bed.

JILLIAN HAD NEVER made love with an unselfish lover. She was only just realizing that right now as she lay across Jack's big bed, waiting for him. He was so tall, so powerful, a man broad of shoulders and muscled to the point of glory. A glimpse of him below the waist, thick and hard and beautiful, and oh, so ready, gave her pause. Jack had taken care of her needs first. He'd been generous and loving and sexy as hell as he brought her to completion. No man had ever put her first like that. No man had ever been this generous in bed. Not that she'd had many lovers, less than she could count on one hand, but the last one, Enrique, had been arrogant, so full of himself, that he'd taken what he'd wanted first and foremost without giving her needs consideration. She'd been a fool where Enrique was concerned. And she wouldn't waste another thought on him, not when Jack was approaching the bed, all Adonis beauty and grace.

Nothing about this man made her timid. In fact, she was as bold as she had ever been whenever she was with Jack and tonight was no exception. She could be generous too. She rose up on her knees and Jack's brows lifted, the expression on his face of surprise and… hope.

She touched his chest first, gazing up into his eyes, holding his stare as she explored, her palms flattening on the tight planes, the deep sea of muscle that rippled under her fingertips. She breathed in a musky all-male scent emanating from his skin as she grazed over his body inch by inch.

Then she sat down, her rear end on her legs and took hold of Jack and his gasp of anticipation echoed in her ears. She wanted this. She wanted to touch him and bring him pleasure too. There had been too many fantasies about him to warrant any hesitation on her part. She stroked him, earning her a grunt from deep down in his throat. Her hand covered his shaft and moved ever so slowly, measuring his ample size, sliding, gliding, stroking. He leaned way back and she molded her hand around his base, positioned herself and took him inside her mouth.

"Fuck yeah." He hissed and she smiled inside, loving this wilder, looser Jack, the rule breaker.

His hand threaded through her hair as he guided her until he was grunting loudly and then finally he'd stilled and immediately backed away. "Lay down, baby. Or this is gonna end quickly."

The desperation in his tone was clear; she was feeling it too. She made herself comfy on his bed, reaching up for him. He was busy wrapping himself in a condom and, once through, he joined her on the bed. Taking her hands in his, he bent his head and kissed her thoroughly. Their tongues mated and played havoc with each other, and then he was kissing her cheek, her chin, her shoulder. His mouth moved to her breasts and he lapped at them, leaving sweet moisture on the very tight budding tips. His legs moved between hers in a parting motion she was only too willing to allow.

"It's been a long time coming, Jillian," he said softly.

"And worth the wait, Jack," she answered, lifting her hips and urging him forward.

"Jillian." He breathed out and then he breached her entrance, filling her full, his cock taut and hard inside her.

She closed her eyes to the beauty of that, of finally joining their bodies. It was as if she'd waited her entire lifetime for this moment and it felt amazing and glorious and right. And he hadn't even moved yet. He hadn't done anything but unite them.

"So damn perfect," he said through tight lips.

Keeping her pinned to the bed, his one hand covering hers above her head, he kissed her again and again. Her heart pounded like a jackhammer, the thudding sounds reaching her ears. She loved being trapped in his embrace, being at his mercy. She trusted him and anything he would do to her.

And then began to thrust, slowly at first. And, oh, already the walls of her body were beginning to give way, to coil into something powerful, to feel every shred of sensation. She moved with him, in rhythm to his deliberate precise grind. He was above her, surrounding her, his presence all consuming.

"Jack, Jack." She wanted to squirm and wiggle, ask for more, but he wasn't going to rush this. He was savoring her body, making it last, making it good. He wasn't taking only what he wanted from her, he was making love to her.

The distinction would eventually break her heart. When she had to leave him.

And then, he picked up the pace thrusting her harder, lifting her ass to get a better angle, to make her feel more, to make her enjoy more and all other thoughts emptied from her head. Jack was in the zone, and she was right there with him.

Until the very end as they both reached for the highest ground and cried out. Their bodies rocked and rolled at the same time, their powerful shuddering release coming in mind-blowing unison.

And then there was silence. A quiet that let her absorb what just happened. To let her recoup some of her spent energy and say farewell to every highly sensitive sensation leaving her.

Jack was probably doing the same.

"Damn," he finally said, in awe, but also with a hint of regret. As if he knew what they had here, wasn't destined to last. As if he knew, this was a fleeting union of bodies and hearts. That their paths were headed in two different directions.

"Damn," she uttered too. Bittersweet emotions threatened to break the spell. She wasn't ready to do that. She wasn't ready to concede the night.

Jack climbed off of her, and then she was being swept up into his arms and curled into his body on the bed. He held her close and kissed her forehead several times.

"After tonight, your rules and conditions don't apply," Jack said in his lawman voice.

It was sorta sweet that he used that tone, as if unequivocally admitting he had no willpower when it came to her and that there was no need for further discussion. If she disagreed with him, she'd fight him on the point, but he was right. After tonight, how could they go back to pretending they weren't hot for each other? How could she possibly live with the man, and not want a repeat performance night after night? "Do you think that's wise?"

"Hell no. It's not wise."

"But necessary?"

He lifted above her, elbows braced on the bed and lowered his mouth to hers. And when the kiss ended, he stared into her eyes. "Touch me," he said.

She knew what he meant, where he wanted her to touch him.

"Jack."

"Do it."

She touched his shaft, already thick and fully aroused again. A shudder thudded through her. She wanted him again too.

Satisfied he'd made his point, he said, "Necessary, babe."

And so, not wise.

Chapter Seven

"THIS IS A pretty one, Jillian," Maddie said, lifting a wedding gown from a dressing rack, the plastic bag crinkling as she brought it in view. "Ivory lace and look at that sweetheart neckline."

Jillian hated to burst Maddie's bubble while standing in the middle of Brides Galore and Much More, surrounded by wall-to-wall wedding gowns and a saleswoman at the ready in case Jillian nodded in approval. "Uh, it is pretty but maybe a bit too much for a small ceremony. There's a lot of lace there."

"Spoken by a woman who deals in lace all day long." Maddie teased, but relented and put the dress back.

Jillian laughed. "You're right. But that's lace in the right place."

Maddie grinned and the saleswoman stepped forward. "Perhaps I can show you something in a little simpler design?"

"Yes," Jillian said, offering Maddie some sympathy.

So far, Maddie had pointed out half a dozen dresses and Jillian had loved every single one, including the lace gown her new friend had just put away, but she couldn't let on that she loved satin or lace or sequins. If she had to wear a gown for her faux wedding, it needed to be simple and understated. She didn't want it to scream permanence. She didn't want a gown that said, *I'll love you forever or you're my soul mate*. Because it was all one big fat lie. And fooling her friends, Maddie recently included, was bad enough without adding more deception to the mix. "I think that's best."

Maddie's shoulders slumped. "At least I talked you out of buying a plain old white suit to get married in."

Jillian took hold of her hand. "I can't tell you how much I appreciate you bringing me here, Maddie. I don't have many friends in town and it's fun having you with me." That much was true.

She was having a good time with Maddie Walker. She enjoyed her company and talking about the baby's arrival and all of the plans Maddie and Trey were making to welcome the little one. It was inspiring to see true love in action, something Jillian wasn't much privy to while growing up or in L.A. where it was a rare thing to see couples make it to a happy ending.

"Ah, here's one I think you'll like." The saleslady walked over with a plastic bag doubled over in her arms and when she unfolded it, Jillian took one look and knew she had her dress.

It wasn't fancy or lacy. There were no satin buttons or sequins, no long train, no bustle. The dress was just right for a fake wedding day with no fuss or muss.

"I'll try it on." She didn't dare look at Maddie. She would be cringing. This wasn't the dress of a woman with hopes and dreams and aspirations of a long blissful marriage. Jillian walked straight into the dressing room without pause because to see Maddie's face and the disappointment there, would only reflect her own.

Two nights ago, she and Jack had had move-the-earth sex. It had opened her eyes to what she'd been missing, to what making love was really all about. Jack had done that for her and she would never forget their first night together. But it had left questions in her mind. What should she do now? Should she move into the house? Should she wait until they were married? Would sex be a part of their deal now? Was she to assume that making love with Jack was going to happen every night?

Yesterday morning, he'd rushed out the door giving her a peck on the mouth claiming he was late for work. And he'd texted her that evening, saying he'd been caught up in an investigation and not to wait up for him. She hadn't. She'd gone back to the guesthouse to sleep.

So it was still unclear where they would proceed from here.

Carefully, she stepped into the dress and as the saleswoman named Bonnie zipped her up, she took a look at herself in the mirror and nodded. "This will do."

"Oh, hon. It shouldn't just do," Bonnie said. "We'll

dress it up with just the right short veil and some jewelry. The gown is actually quite becoming."

"I agree," Maddie said, peeking into the dressing room. "It's very pretty."

It was pretty, she couldn't disagree with either of them, the dress had classic lines. "It fits well and that's the main thing," she said, brightening her dreary comment with a smile. "I'll take it."

Clearly, Bonnie was anxious to make the sale since she didn't try to talk her into trying on something else. "Wonderful. Would you like to take it with you?"

"If you wouldn't mind holding on to it, I'll come back later today to pick it up."

"Sure."

After Jillian settled up with the saleswoman, she slipped her arm through Maddie's as they walked out of the shop. "Mission accomplished. I have a dress. And I owe it all to you."

"Gosh, Jillian. I hope I wasn't pressuring you too much in there. I tend to get a bit romantic and sentimental about these things. The dress you picked is really nice."

"It's fitting for the occasion and don't feel badly. I'm happy to have your help. So how about we go to lunch?"

"Of course. Baby Walker is grumbling in there, he wants to be fed."

"He?"

"Or she. We don't know the sex of the baby yet."

"Well then we'd better get the little one fed right away."

They stopped at a recently opened outdoor restaurant that Maddie wanted to try. The new chef was friendly and eager for business and made them feel right at home. The food was amazing, a fusion of French and southwest cuisine. They spent time praising the food, getting to know each other better and laughing at silly things. Jillian wiped her mouth with the napkin one final time after both of their plates were cleared. "Do you have just a few more minutes today?" she asked Maddie. "I have a surprise for you."

"Oh, uh, yes. I have time." Caught off guard, Maddie leaned forward, arching her brows. "What kind of surprise?"

Jillian smiled. "If I told you, it wouldn't be a surprise. Come and take a walk with me."

"Okay, I'm game."

Ten minutes later, they were entering Barely There Express and Maddie took a good long look around. "Jillian, the place is already shaping up."

"It's amazing what a few structural changes and a coat of paint can do. I'm pleased so far, but more work has to be done before I can open the shop. I've got inventory in the back room and as soon as the new floors and windows are installed, the shelving will go up and the rounders will be put in place."

"All this, an engagement party in two days, and then a wedding. You've got your hands full, my friend."

My friend. A quick bout of emotion rocked her insides.

She and Maddie were becoming friends and it felt so darn good to know that someone in this town had her back. Jillian already felt the same about Maddie; she hoped to always be her friend. "I'm used to being busy," she said.

But she wouldn't admit to Maddie or anyone else that she wished this whole wedding fiasco was over so she could settle into some sort of life in Hope Wells, without incident, until the year was up.

"Well, yeah. I guess so." Maddie smiled. "If you want something done, ask a busy person."

"That could be said about you too, Mads. You're having a baby, running a vet practice and throwing a wedding, all at the same time."

"I guess, we're not too different, are we?"

"Nope, great minds and all that. Have a seat and I'll be back in one second." Maddie sat on one of the two folding chairs scattered about the room. "Where are you going?"

"To get your surprise," she called over her shoulder.

Jillian walked into the backroom and came out with a box wrapped in lavender ribbon printed with her company logo, the words *Barely There* forming an arrow in italics going through a heart-shaped icon. She dragged a folding chair over to where Maddie sat and took a seat beside her.

She handed her the box. "This is for you."

"Me?" Maddie glanced at the box.

Jillian had to admit that her design and logo, the whole package, was truly elegant and beautiful and captured her brand perfectly. Pride filled her up inside whenever she offered a gift to someone special and today was no exception.

"Open it, please."

"You do know I'm four months pregnant."

"Open it, Maddie. You'll see I haven't forgotten that little fact."

Maddie undid the ribbon, folding it up nicely as if she didn't want to damage it, and then lifted the box lid. Thin lacy lavender tissue paper protected the contents and Maddie spread it apart carefully.

She looked inside the box, then up at Jillian, blinking her eyes. "It's gorgeous. But I…"

"It's from my Baby There collection. Pregnant mommies still want to look pretty in their nightclothes and sexy for their men."

Maddie lifted out the silky cream-colored garment, a beautiful compliment to Maddie's auburn hair and skin tone. A sheet of black lace material attached to the bra cups covered the mother's baby bump to below the navel, just barely and allowed for quite a bit of skin to show in the back and along the sides. If pregnancy could be sexy, this was the ticket, with panties to match.

"I love it, Jillian. Did you design this?"

"I did. I wanted my collection to include all women, young, old, pregnant, timid, and not so timid."

Maddie laughed. "This must be from the not so timid pregnancy line. I think Trey's gonna have heart palpitations when I come to bed wearing this."

"That's the idea."

Maddie leaned over and gave her a hug. "Thank you."

"You're very welcome, Maddie." And Jillian locked their embrace, holding onto her friend for extra beats of a minute, choking up a little bit inside. Before emotion got the better of her, she broke away and plastered on a smile. "And you can tell Trey, I said you're welcome to him too."

THE KNOCK ON the guesthouse door came at precisely seven o'clock that evening. Jillian had just kicked off her flip-flops and curled herself up on the sofa, ready to hunker down and go over the latest inventory stats Tessa had emailed today. Removing her computer from her lap, she padded over to the door, peeked through the peephole, and found Jack standing there. He was wearing his uniform and, heaven help her, looking deliciously sexy. She swallowed a gulp of air, begging for better control of her emotions. It wasn't coming fast enough and when Jack knocked again, she jumped from the force of his knocks.

"Coming," she said, waiting one more beat to get hold of herself.

She opened the door and smiled. "Hello, Jack."

He took a leisurely stroll over her body, his eyes darkening as they lingered on her breasts. *I'm up here buddy*, she wanted to say, but in all honesty she was turned on by his unabashed admiration. Jack didn't have to do much to get her going. Just a look would do.

"Hi."

"What can I do for you?"

His brows rose and his pupils nearly turned black. "I could make a few suggestions."

She just might want to hear them. "Um, I was looking over some files. Checking inventory stats. Boring stuff. Would you like to come in?"

He kept his eyes on her, all that deep dark intensity aimed her way. "I've got pizza and beer at the house."

"What kind of pizza?"

"Your favorite."

"You don't know my favorite."

"I think I know what you like," he said in a rough voice, leaning his body against the doorframe. From under his sheriff shirt, muscles were bulging.

She chewed on her bottom lip. They weren't really talking about pizza anymore. "You haven't ordered yet, have you?"

He gave his head half a shake. "So what is it?"

"Pineapple."

He made a face and she laughed. "But I love pepperoni too."

"Twenty minutes?"

"I'll be there."

He gave her body another once over, then pointed up and down, drawing an invisible line through the air. "I like the look."

She blinked. She was wearing gray sweatpants and a matching sleeveless tank. No makeup, her hair in a messy bun at the top of her head. "Uh, thanks. I think."

He grinned and walked away, giving her an excellent view of his broad shoulders and perfect ass. They were going to have crazy raw sex again tonight and there was nothing she could do to stop it. Not that she wanted to. A pulse beat hard against her neck as she imagined undressing the sheriff. She wanted to call him back and tell him not to change out of his uniform, but he was already out of sight.

Darn.

Half an hour later, Jillian bit into a slice of pizza and a string of mozzarella cheese attached to her mouth like a retractable clothesline. "Yum, this is delicious." She cupped her hand under her chin to catch any stray cheese that she might miss.

Jack sipped from a beer bottle and nodded. "Hits the spot."

He'd already downed his first piece and was going in for another. She was grateful they were sitting in Jack's kitchen and having a conversation without ripping each other's clothes off. Though Jack's eyes were constantly on her and her nerves were bouncing despite the fact that he'd changed into a pair of washed-out Wranglers and white tee, squashing her sheriff in uniform fantasy. Yet, she had the feeling he was refraining from jumping her bones deliberately.

"You know," he began, after chewing and swallowing half a piece of pizza in one gigantic bite, "after the engagement party, you should move in here."

It was inevitable. She had to move in with Jack to keep up appearances. "But shouldn't we do that after we, uh, get married?"

Jack's face didn't contort this time when she mentioned their upcoming marriage. It was some sort of progress. Maybe he liked the idea of having a temporary wife and bed partner, without the usual strings. "I think it'll look more realistic if you moved in on Sunday, after we make the engagement official."

She shrugged. This was his game and she had to play by his rules. "I can do that."

"And I also think you should meet Beau." She noted indecision in his eyes for a moment, before he set his jaw firm to the idea.

"I'd like that."

"The last thing I want is for the boy to be hurt. He's had enough shit happens, for one lifetime. I, uh, we have to handle this carefully."

"Whatever you say, Jack."

"Whatever I say?" He repeated, his voice taking a bitter tone. "Woman, I don't know what the hell is right anymore. I don't know if all of this is one big colossal mistake. I don't know what'll happen with Beau, if I'll even be granted the adoption. But, it won't be for lack of trying, that's for damn sure."

"I understand you're worried."

He stared at her for a fraction of a second, his eyes revealing the turmoil in his soul. Then he shoved his plate away, stood up and ran his hands through his hair. "Damn you, Jillian."

She wasn't shocked at his accusation. She was to blame for the whole dilemma and she wasn't about to defend herself. She'd acted selfishly, coming here, expecting Jack to go along with her little scheme, without giving a thought to his own problems, to how it might affect his life.

She stood and walked over to him. "I know this is my fault, Jack. I'm trying to help, but if—"

He shook his head. "It's not that, babe. It's not that at all. Why do you always assume I'm mad at you?"

She smiled. "Because you usually are."

"Yeah, well, that's because I'm having a hard time with—"

"Trying to make all the right decisions for everyone. It's what you do, Jack. It's who you are."

He scoffed and shook his head. "That's not what I was going to say."

"Then what?"

Instead of answering her, he grabbed both of her wrists forcefully and pulled her so close she had no option but to stare straight into his deep dark intense eyes.

She blinked, once, twice. "Are you going to arrest me?"

The comment cracked his stony face. "I am so screwed," he said, and then lowered his mouth and claimed her lips.

The kiss caught her off-guard and, for a moment, she just stood there enjoying the taste of beer and pizza on his breath, but before long, his hands were dipping under her tank top and inching up her torso. Tiny whimpers tore from her throat.

"I like your sounds," he murmured over her lips. "Can't get enough."

"That's on you." She breathed, before kissing him back. "You, ah—" And then his hands were on her breasts, cupping the globes over her thin, lacy black bra. She loved the feel of his hands on her, the way his palms flattened and absorbed every bit of her. "You make me totally… breathless."

He unfastened her bra and somehow managed to lift it and her tank over her head. She was bare from the waist up and Jack didn't waste a minute, lowering his head to kiss her breasts, nip at her skin, use his tongue to work magic, and now she was moaning, her body pulsing with need.

He abandoned her breasts for a moment to pull down her remaining clothes and after she stepped out of them, he was kissing her again, making her squirm when he brought one hand to the apex of her thighs. He spread his hand out wide, parting her legs and used his palm to apply pressure to her sensitive folds, to make her feel, want, crave. Then he slid his hand back and forth, up and down against her delicate skin and she jumped, hissing out a breath.

"Hold onto me." He ground out.

And she obeyed, wrapping both arms around his neck, her fingertips buried deep into his shoulder blades. Jack's kisses were fiery hot, branding her, his tongue sweeping through, making her crazy while down below, she was burning, burning. His palm pressed her deep and she couldn't hold back another second. She shattered, her body spasms coming quick and hard.

"Jack, oh, wow," she cried and then her sounds became unintelligible, soft moans that echoed inside the room.

He was holding her firm from behind now, squeezing her butt cheeks, making sure she felt every last rocking sensation whirling through her at the speed of sound.

And when it was over, she fell limp into his arms, her head tucked into his chest.

He picked her up under her legs and carried her straight to his bedroom.

SOMETIME AFTER MIDNIGHT, Jillian woke up in Jack's bed, his arm slung possessively over her waist. She was wearing her birthday suit and so was he, a glorious gift of male virility that, for the time being, was all hers. That in itself was a problem. She couldn't seem to say no to Jack, not when it came to getting naked.

They'd made love until both had completely run out of steam. During the course of the night, they'd scorched the sheets leaving the other with absolutely no complaints. Jack's praise had assured her of that. Her body was sore, in the very best way and now that she was fully awake, her mind was reacting to what had happened, to what Jack meant to say to her before she'd cracked his armor with her little joke.

A hand brushed her hair aside and Jack's nose nestled into her neck. He planted a few lazy kisses there and whispered in her ear. "I didn't tire you out?"

She smiled. "Do you have amnesia? Of course you did."

"So why are you awake?"

"Why are you?" she tossed back at him.

Instead of making a joke, he sighed heavily.

She turned around from their spooning position to face him. "Tell me. What did you want to say to me earlier?"

Through the dim filter of moonlight streaming into the room, she caught his somber expression. "It can wait."

"Jack?"

"Babe, you're beautiful. You're naked. And you're in my bed. Do you really expect my brain to function?"

She made a production of pulling at the sheets enough to wrap herself up like a burrito, covering her body from view. "There, now I'm not naked." She rose, rather stumbled from the bed. "And, now, I'm no longer in your bed."

Jack sat up, dumbfounded. Scratching his head, he sighed again. "You don't have to get out of bed." He reached out to snag her hand, giving her a gentle tug. She fell back on the bed. "I want you here. Ah, hell."

He rose, and all those muscles, from his legs to his torso to his bulging biceps, caught her eye. He was beautiful and at the moment, covering it all up with a pair of trousers and a t-shirt. Once clothed, he took a seat beside her on the bed and stared straight out the window. "I meant it when I said we can't hurt Beau. We have to be very careful. We both know how this is going to end in a year's time, but he doesn't. He's innocent in our little charade." Jack faced her now, his eyes sharp and determined. "I guess what I'm asking, is for you to be sure to not get emotionally involved."

"You mean with Beau?"

He stared into her eyes and blinked, before nodding. Oh, God, he meant with him too. He was warning her off, telling her he wasn't capable of loving her again. Even while in her head, she was wondering if they couldn't make this crazy thing work. Even, if for just a moment in time, she was starting to believe that her life here with Jack could be a fantasy come true. Silly of her to wish it. To hope.

"We have to appear to be a happy family, without really being one. It sucks and I hate every second of this, Jillian."

She took a gulp of air. She knew her role in this deception, but having it laid out to her this way was brutal. She wasn't a mechanical robot. She wasn't a woman without a soul. Her feelings and emotions were all wrapped up in this. He wasn't deliberately trying to cut her to the quick, but it hurt like hell, anyway.

"I don't think I can live under the same roof with you and keep my hands off," he admitted.

"That's what you meant when you said, 'I am so screwed'."

"God, Jillian, I'm not gonna lie. Having sex with you complicates things. But there's no way around it. We're gonna be living together, getting married. And I... unless you tell me otherwise, I do want you in my bed. Every night. Maybe that's not fair, but..."

Why deprive themselves of a mutually satisfying affair, in the interim? That was what he was implying. And Jillian had to ask herself that, as well. Jack was someone she respected. He was a good man who had shown her what making love should be like. He was hot and sexy and, lately, the star of every version of her fondest fantasies. But could she really do this? Have scorching hot sex with this man on a regular basis, pretend to be his wife, pretend to be a family, when all of this would eventually end?

It was what she'd signed up for. She'd given Jack her promise. She was in this to the bitter end, and all she had to do on a daily basis was remind herself it was all temporary. It wasn't real. The only objective was to insure that Jack adopt Beau.

"Jillian?" Jack was watching her carefully. He was wondering if he'd gone too far, if he'd given her a bit too much reality for the middle of the night. She could see all of that insecurity, along with deep regret, in his eyes.

"I'm here, Jack. I'm not going back on my word. But tonight, I am going back to my own bed, in the guesthouse."

"Jillian, babe." The plea in his voice didn't deter her.

"It's okay, Jack. It's my choice and I think it's for the best."

"It's always gonna be your choice," he added.

Yeah, he would never force her to do anything. Jack wasn't made that way, but she couldn't spend the rest of the night in his bed. Not tonight. Ice cold water had been poured onto her soul. And she was frozen inside.

She needed time to process all of this.

Because Jack was right about one thing, having sex did complicate an already tricky situation.

THE NEXT DAY, Jack set a hand on Beau's shoulder guiding him to a café table in the corner of Giggles and Cream. The boy's eyes bugged out as he took in the ice cream parlor that also doubled for a candy and toy store. The shop filled with colorful stuffed animals, rainbow lollipops and chocolates was everything a child could ever dream about.

"Let's sit down," Jack said, "and you can decide what flavors of ice cream you want."

Beau's face lit up even brighter. "Do I get more than one?"

"As many flavors as you like. Only because you ate a good lunch."

"Oh, boy."

They each took a seat, Jack facing the entrance of the shop keeping an eye out for Jillian.

Last night he'd invited her to Giggles and Cream after lunch today for ice cream to meet Beau. Jack had the afternoon off and whenever he could arrange it, he liked to spend his free time with the boy. He wouldn't blame Jillian if she begged off after all the crap he'd given her yesterday, but she'd texted him this morning, she would be here.

He'd been a goddamn idiot with Jillian and hurt her in the process, making her feel like that young girl from the wrong side of town again. She'd never admit that to him, but he knew, he'd witnessed it in the sad, injured look in her eyes. Had seen the slump of her shoulders today as he watched from his front window when Jillian had climbed into her car and driven off this morning. He'd only been honest with her, but he could have done better, much better, and put his cautious words in softer terms. He meant only to set some boundaries and instead he'd managed to put up mile high walls.

Beau kicked his legs under the table and fidgeted in his seat, keeping himself occupied the way eager little boys did, making Jack smile. And then Jillian walked in. Jack saw her before she found them and he rose as she sashayed across the floor, searching. The second her pretty baby blues found him, his breath froze in his throat. He was momentarily stunned. She'd changed her clothes for the ice cream date and looked gorgeous wearing a cotton candy pink and white polka dot sundress, her hair pulled into a high ponytail, Barbie style, and looked very much like she belonged on the menu at Giggles and Cream. An edible delight. Her smile was so wide, so forgiving, that Jack nearly tripped over his own boots walking over to her.

"Hi," he said. "I'm glad you made it."

"Hi," she said back, peering over his shoulder to where Beau sat. "I wouldn't disappoint Beau."

He nodded and took her hand, refusing to read anything into her comment as they approached the table.

Jillian didn't wait for introductions. She simply leaned down, hands on knees and looked at Beau. "Hi there. I'm Jillian. I've heard so much about you, Beau. Do you mind if I have ice cream with you?"

The boy smiled. "Do you get to have as many flavors as you want too?"

Jillian bobbed her head up and down. "Oh, I think so."

"Because you ate a good lunch?"

She glanced at Jack, and he grinned back at her. "Yes, I did eat a good lunch too." She put out her hand and Beau slid his smaller one in hers. "Nice to meet you, Beau." They pumped a few times and then Jillian straightened.

"Can we have ice cream now?" the boy asked Jack, climbing out of his seat.

"Sure thing."

The three of them walked over to the counter and it took some doing to pick from twenty-two flavors. Jack bought Beau an adult-sized waffle cone, dipped in chocolate and covered in sprinkles and let the boy pick out five flavors. He'd never eat it all, but that wasn't the point. Today was all about indulging the boy and having fun.

They took their seats and Jack put a napkin around Beau's neck for spillage. Jillian licked at her strawberry chip ice cream cone, her tongue darting in and out wrapping around the cone and Jack gave himself shit for allowing his mind to anywhere not G-rated. He focused on the child.

"Beau, Jillian and I are going to be married in a couple of weeks. We both would like you to come to our wedding. Monty will be there too and a few other friends."

"And it's going to be on a ranch with lots of horses and cows and, oh, a bunch of other animals," Jillian added.

"That's true and it's all arranged for you to be there," Jack said. "Would you like to come?"

Beau lifted his eyes off his cone and nodded. "Do I get to ride a horse?"

Jack darted a glance at Jillian and she smiled warmly giving him the go ahead to answer. "I think that's possible. After the ceremony."

"Oh, boy, thanks." Happily, Beau resumed his destruction of the cone. Then as a thought seemed to take hold, he stopped in mid-lick to focus his big brown puppy eyes at Jillian. "Does that mean you're gonna be my mommy?"

His innocent question bound Jack up in tight knots. How quickly five-year-old Beau had put two and two together. Jack had spoken to Beau about Jillian once before briefly in vague terms, but the boy surprised him now at how astute he was. Or had it been wishful thinking? Were Beau's hopes and dreams wrapped up in having a family again? A father *and* a mother? The knot in Jack's gut twisted a little tighter.

To Jillian's credit, she didn't hesitate to take hold of the situation. She reached for Beau's hand. "I hope so, Beau. I will be Jack's wife and if all goes as planned, you're going to be a big part of our lives."

"Cool beans," the boy said with a bob of his head and Jack blurted a laugh.

Jillian grinned, connecting with Jack's gaze. "Yeah, cool beans."

And Beau went about the big business of finishing off his waffle cone.

Chapter Eight

IN A TOWN the size of Hope Wells, news of the town hero's engagement party was noteworthy and local journalists and photographers were welcomed to the big bash. The town mayor, Judd O'Brien, strutted in, using the party as a way to make his own headlines, taking handshake photos with Jack and joking about being out of a job if Sheriff Jack Walker ever decided to go into politics.

Jack's mouth immediately detoured south at the suggestion and everyone around them laughed. Jillian stood off to the side with Jack's dad which was probably a mistake because Monty Walker didn't hold back when something was on his mind and damn the consequences. "You look dazzling tonight, Jillie. And the house has never looked better. You got candles glowing inside, lights glowing outside, fine food and drink. I'm impressed. You sure know how to throw a party."

"Thank you, Monty. It wasn't hard putting it together. I really didn't do much but pick up the phone and make the arrangements. Jack busted his butt working on the house this week."

"Yeah, he's a hard worker. You know, you and my boy make a fine couple," he whispered into her ear. "Won't be long before you make this union the *real* thing."

Jillian quickly glanced around, making sure they were truly out of earshot of any partygoers. "Shh, Monty. Please."

"Just saying what's on my mind."

"Well, put it out of your mind. It would never work."

But Monty just kept on talking, "I see my boy seeking you out. Every second he's had free tonight, his eyeballs land on you. That means something and you don't know what *will* work unless you try."

But Jillian did know. Jack had made his feelings clear on the subject. He didn't want to tear open an old wound, when he was still trying to heal from the other injuries in his life. A mother abandoning her family, a fiancée calling it quits. He didn't want a replay of the past and he was protecting his heart. She had firsthand knowledge of that healing process. It was hard, and bitter at times, with no guarantees.

They'd made their pact. Theirs was a win-win bargain and they were to keep any personal involvement to a minimum. It sounded simple on paper, but living the deception wasn't quite so easy.

All she had to do was look at Jack and her heart began to flutter. Dressed in a slate gray two-piece suit, the collar of his shirt open, devoid of a tie, he rivaled any male cover model in elegance and sex appeal. Women eyed him openly. She couldn't blame them; Jack was a man who could make a girl giddy. Most men admired him too; he had a sense of sarcastic humor that put smiles on faces. Jack had no idea his influence in this town. He had no idea, how highly regarded he was. Pride filled her up inside, spreading out and overtaking the rational layers of good sense that kept her heart protected and her head on straight.

Don't get caught up in the emotion of the day.

It was true that Jack met her eyes several times tonight, but only to see if she was owning up to her part of the ruse. He was checking in, making sure she was playing her role.

Jillian spotted Ella milling about, looking a little lost and eyeing the front door as a means of escape. Jillian wasn't going to let that happen.

"Will you excuse me for a second, Monty?" she asked and sauntered off in Ella's direction without giving him a chance to respond.

"Ella, hi again!" Jillian grabbed her attention before she could make a run for it.

Two hours ago, Ella had made her delivery and Jillian had urged her to come back for the party. She was thrilled to see that Ella had. And she'd dressed for the occasion, wearing a slimming black dress with a skirt that flared to her knees. The fit took ten pounds off. "You look very nice," she said.

"I haven't dressed up in ages."

"Well, you still have a sense of style, Ella. Just like always." She'd been voted "best dressed" in high school.

"Thanks." But her shoulders caved in as she took in the

surroundings.

Parties used to be her thing, but now she seemed awkwardly uncomfortable. She'd been out of circulation too long, Jillian decided.

"We're getting compliments on your pastries. Everyone is raving."

"Really?"

"They're as tasty as they are beautiful. You're very talented."

"Thanks," she said again, a hint of a smile emerging. "I'm glad you like them. I guess I didn't really congratulate you properly. Congrats. Jack's an awesome guy."

Just then, a group Jack was entertaining burst out laughing, and he was grinning along with them. From the other side of the room, he caught her eye and gave her a little wink.

"You're very lucky," Ella said.

"I, uh, yes. I am."

Jack broke away from the group and walked over. He was quick to curl his arm around Jillian's waist, his fingers digging in possessively and the gesture wasn't lost on her. Warm tingles ran a marathon up and down her spine. Jack greeted Ella by kissing her cheek. "I'm glad you made it."

"Congratulations."

"Thank you. Did Jillian tell you how much everyone is enjoying your pastries? I mean, come on, they're freakin' sinful."

Ella chuckled and her cheeks turned rosy. "You've got a way with words, Jack."

"I mean it. I'm not gonna stick to your maple bars anymore, not that they aren't delicious. But I think the boys at the station would love it if I showed up with a box of those chocolate lava mousse filled thingies."

"Okay, just say the word and I'll have them ready."

"I'm putting my order in now. Next Friday morning at eight. Two dozen and throw in some maple bars too, for the die-hards."

"Gotcha."

Dakota walked up at the same time as Colby Ryan and Jillian found the mix of people in the group fascinating. Day, as Jack had introduced her, definitely had a thing for Jack's good friend, though she was trying her best not to glare daggers at Ella who had managed to snag Colby's attention.

The conversation was lively and Jillian found she was really enjoying getting to know Jack's friends a little better. But the second there was a lull Jack grabbed her hand and nuzzled her throat, sending shockwaves through her body. "You mind if I drag my fiancée off for a little bit?" he asked their guests. "There's something we need to discuss."

"Sure Jack," Colby said, giving them a wink. "*Discuss* away and don't mind us."

Jack gazed lovingly into Jillian's eyes. "Don't worry, we won't."

And the next thing she knew, Jillian was being whisked

away to the mudroom, adjacent to the kitchen. Jack closed the door behind them, and let go a big breath. "How're you holding up? Okay?"

Suddenly, she became aware of how tiny the room was, Jack's presence like a towering redwood in a nursery greenhouse. "Yes, I'm enjoying myself. How about you?"

"I'm hangin' on, babe. It's kinda surreal with all these people here. The house is overflowing. I think half the town showed up."

He was exaggerating, but they had invited over one hundred people. And they all seemed to be here. "It's part of the plan."

Jack met her eyes. "Yeah. The big plan."

"We're doing this for Beau."

"Yeah." Jack rubbed the back of his neck. "About that, I got good news tonight. The judge is gonna make a ruling on the adoption before the month is up."

"That's great news, Jack." And it made all of this seem more worthwhile and less shady. "If you get the okay to adopt Beau, then it'll all be worth it."

"You think so?"

How could he doubt it? The two of them belonged together. Whenever Jack looked at the boy, his eyes beamed in an unmistakable glow of affection and love. "I've seen you together, Jack. That boy idolizes you. You're crazy about him. You two are a good fit."

"Thanks. I guess I need to keep hearing that. Listen, Jillian. About what I said the other night, I was out of line. I didn't mean it the way it came out."

She wouldn't play ignorant. She knew what he was talking about. It was the giant elephant in the room. "It's fine, Jack. You pulled a Monty. And you're forgiven."

"A Monty?" All seriousness left Jack's face and something in his eyes twinkled. "You know, you say it like it is, blunt and brutal, but always the truth."

"Well, hell."

"You two are related, you know."

"Don't remind me," he said, but with a smile.

He took both of her hands then and looked deep into her eyes. "I know this isn't easy on you."

"It's not so hard, Walker. If I have to be hitched to someone, you're as good a candidate as I'm going to find."

"That so?" He squeezed her hands.

"Yeah, you spruce up nicely too."

"Jillian," he said, drawing her closer, pressing his mouth to her ear. "And you, in that dress, are fucking gorgeous tonight. Pardon my language, but I can't keep my eyes off you."

Her body heated instantly. Hearing Jack speak that way, turned her on. He was upstanding and good and honest, but with her, he seemed to let down his guard. He was more himself around her than he might even realize.

And she was glad he liked what she'd chosen to wear. She'd wondered earlier, what he'd think about her putting on a sleeveless cherry red form-fitting dress that flowed to the floor. It wasn't indecent by any standards, yet the dress didn't hide the shape of her body and only helped accentuate her full chest and deep curves in lacy chiffon. She'd painted her lips a rosy red and wore matching shoes and had given freedom to her long blonde waves. "Jack," she whispered back.

He spread his hands on her waist, pulling her closer and, just as his mouth would give her a taste, the door opened.

"Whoops, sorry to interrupt." It was Jack's pal, Colby, a smart smirk on his face contradicting his claim of apology. "I was sent on a mission to find you. Your dad is about ready to give a toast."

Jack blinked. "A toast?"

"Yeah, you know, a toast to the happy couple, where you listen to wonderful things about yourselves and then clink fancy glasses and down champagne."

"Yes, don't you remember, Jack." Jillian intervened, drawing his attention by meeting his eyes and prodding. "Your dad mentioned it today and we thought it was a great idea."

"Oh, yeah, right."

Jack went along with her, as this was the first either of them had heard anything about Monty giving them a toast. "Well, we'd better get out there. Our guests are waiting," she said, tugging Jack's hand and marching him away from the mudroom and his grinning friend.

JACK STOOD NEXT to Jillian, their arms around each other's waists, facing the guests that were packed into the patio, champagne flutes well in hand. His father's mouth was moving and he was saying all the right things and, for a minute, Jack fell into the charade and imagined what life would be like with Jillian by his side. He pictured them as they were yesterday, eating ice cream, chatting it up with Beau, laughing and having fun. A family.

But Jack had to protect Beau. It was his first priority. And entering into such dreams was asking for trouble. Beau had lost too much already. And, if Jack were honest, so had he. He'd never gotten over his mother's abandonment, though no one ever spoke about it. Monty's heart had been broken when his wife decided she didn't want to be hitched to a lawman in a small town. She'd taken off for bigger and better things, heading to New York to pursue her dreams and one six-year-old little boy had lost his mother.

Jack looked at Jillian standing beside him, as beautiful as she'd always been and any man would find it impossible not to think of the possibilities with her. Especially now, as her unique flowery scent wafted to his nose and wisps of her honey blonde hair brushed his shoulders.

Side-by-side, at one time in their lives, they'd thought they could have it all.

But who was he kidding? Jillian was, and had always

been, determined to make her own way in the world. If her company hadn't fallen on hard times, she wouldn't even be here. She hadn't come back for him. It was something he reminded himself daily. Once she was done saving her company, once her year was up, she'd leave. He had no doubt. It was what he was counting on and what he feared the most. How crazy was that?

"And I know the future is bright for my son, Jack, and his new fiancée, Jillian. If ever I felt something deep in my heart, it's that these two belong together. They deserve happiness and now it's theirs for the taking now. So, raise your glass, to Jack and Jillie and wish them a lifetime of love."

Jack smiled for the guests and touched his glass to Jillian's. Meeting her gaze above the rim, they both sipped from the flutes as glasses clinked around them. With everyone's eyes on them, he dipped his head and planted a kiss on her soft champagne soaked lips. It was the kiss he meant to give her in the privacy of the mudroom, the kiss he'd been dying to give her after watching her eat ice cream yesterday. Someone came up to remove the glasses from their hands, freeing him up so that he could encircle her waist, draw her closer and deepen the kiss.

The guests oohed and ahhed and applause broke out.

Jack ended the kiss sooner than he wanted and pulled slightly back. Jillian gave him one solid look, her eyes widening for an instant, before she turned toward the crowd of well-wishers and laughed.

Jack hugged her to his waist, in a show of unity. "Thank you for the toast, Dad, and thank you all for coming. Jillian and I, well, we appreciate you all being here to share in this celebration."

"WE DID IT," Jack whispered to Jillian two hours later. The party was dying down and only a few guests lingered. "We are officially engaged."

"And Hope Wells has a new story to tell," Jillian said.

There would be photos in the newspapers, with far better captions than the last time he and Jillian had been photographed. Hopefully, their damage control had worked. "Yeah," Jack said, nodding.

The sound of glass cracking against the wood floor interrupted Jack's next thought and he turned in that direction. Dakota tugged on her hair and giggled, standing in a puddle of champagne. "Oops. The g-glass slipped outta my hand. S-sorry."

She staggered toward the fireplace, one wobbly foot touching down after the other. She finally gripped the edge and held on, leaning heavily. Before Jack could make a move, Colby was there, in her face. "Day, damnit. You've had too much to drink."

"Have not. It's only a small buzz, Cole."

"You're hammered."

"I am *not* hammered," she shot back.

"Day? What's gotten into you tonight? You've been—"

"Shut up, Cole. You're not my boss tonight. J-Jack is Colby Ryan my b-boss tonight? Can h-he tell me what to do in your home?"

Jack pressed his lips together. Oh, boy, Day was going to give it to Colby and maybe that's just what the guy needed, a swift kick in the ass. "No Day. Cole's not your boss here. You're a guest in my home."

"Thanks, pal." Colby shot him a look. "Can't you see she's had too much to drink?"

"Don't you dare t-talk over me, Cole. I'm right here, I can h-hear you."

"Crap, Dakota. C'mon, it's time to go home. I'll drive you."

He took her hand and she immediately yanked it free, leaving Colby confounded. "I'm not r-ready to go home yet."

"Oh, you are so ready."

"You wouldn't know when a gal's ready for anything." And then she mumbled something that sounded like *you jerk*.

"What does that even mean?" he asked.

Another mumble from Dakota and Colby turned to him again, a question in his eyes.

Jack shrugged. He wasn't touching this one. He had

enough to contend with right now with his own female problems.

Jillian walked over to Dakota, bypassing Colby and put a hand on her arm. "Would you like to sit down in the kitchen with me? I was just about to have a cup of coffee. I'll get you a cup too."

Dakota glared at Colby, folded her arms over her middle, and nodded to Jillian. "That would be nice."

And on her way out, she turned to Colby, suddenly appearing sober as a Sunday morning minister. "I'm not an idiot, I won't be driving tonight and I don't need a ride from you."

Colby frowned. "But I'm passing right by your place, I can drop you off."

Dakota shook her head. "No thanks."

And with that, she lifted her head sky-high and walked out the door with Jillian by her side, a slight wobble in her step.

"What in hell just happened?" Colby asked him.

Jack sighed. "Did I overhear you inviting Ella to the ranch?"

"Yeah, she mentioned she hadn't ridden in years. I offered to take her riding one day. No big deal, right?"

Jack sighed. "Wrong. But I'm going to let you figure it out for yourself, greenhorn."

"Greenhorn? Hell, I know more about horses than you have brain cells, Walker."

"Yeah, but you know even less than I do about women. And with that, I rest my case."

Monday morning, Jillian was back at work in her shop, going over her progress with Brett. He'd labored this past week including the weekend and the result of his hard work was evident. New shelves had been installed as well as marble counters and below them a few sets of easy slide drawers had been constructed. They only needed a coat of paint.

The cash register was at the back of the store, along with a DIY espresso counter. Freebies always brought in customers and more times than not, they usually wound up making a purchase. Besides, Jillian liked the idea of offering the guests in her shop a cup of coffee. She wanted the experience in Barely There to be a positive one, even though Hope Wells hadn't exactly welcomed her home with open arms. At least, the newspaper articles on their engagement today had been kind, most likely due to Jack's sterling reputation in this town.

She'd already been visited by a few gossipmongers, stopping by the shop to offer congratulations and see her brand new engagement ring. She'd given each one of them a tour of the place, never once breaking her smile and extending them another invitation to return for her soft opening, which would be in a few weeks and was met by surprise and finally, some degree of approval.

"Baby steps," she said to Brett.

He smiled. "I wouldn't worry over it. You're gonna do well here."

"How can you tell?"

"This place is gonna rock it. Sure, you'll get a tad bit of badmouthing by some, but your shop is a shiny new penny in Hope Wells and it's gonna attract a herd of customers."

"That's the plan anyway."

The *plan?* Jillian seemed to always have a plan and most of them had panned out, except for when they didn't. And it was those plans-gone-awry that had caused her the most trouble. She was hoping to reverse her recent bad karma and offer something unique and engaging to the town.

"This new shop and a new husband soon, Miss Lane. Seems your plans are working out just fine," Brett said, giving her a wink, and then heaved a massive shelf over his shoulder like it was a toy block. Muscles bunched and pulled as he walked past her and into the backroom.

Brett was a charmer, that was for sure and that wink probably worked on ninety-nine percent of the Hope Wells female population. But Jillian had Jack on the brain lately. She'd moved into the main house yesterday as a newly engaged woman and with the wedding just two weeks away, she supposed all was going well.

Yesterday, she'd taken up residence in Jack's guest room in the main house and had turned in early, well before he'd come home from a late shift. She'd heard him enter through the garage and, minutes later, his footfalls stopped just outside her closed door. She felt his presence behind her door and her heart stilled, beating so darn fast in her chest she could hear the pounding up in her ears and only once he'd moved on, did her breathing calm again.

It was crazy. She was a grown woman playing cat and mouse games with her fake fiancé, but his warning kept getting into her head.

Don't get emotionally involved.

She wouldn't. She couldn't.

She only hoped it wasn't too late.

The new doorbell chimed, announcing a visitor, and Jillian's head snapped up. Dakota Jennings walked in carrying a bunch of whimsical wildflowers. Her pretty face was downcast and sullen.

"Hello," she said walking over, wearing jeans and a chambray shirt. Her black hair was roped into a long braid going down her back. "I hope I'm not disturbing you."

"Not at all, Dakota. It's good to see you. Is everything okay?"

The girl shook her head. "No, nothing's okay. I'm here to apologize to you about the other night. I'm so sorry I made a scene. I usually don't drink like that, but I... well, I am so sorry if I ruined your engagement party."

"Oh, Dakota, you didn't ruin a thing. Honestly. Jack and I were worried about you, though."

"I know. I just left the sheriff's office. I apologized to him too. He's such a good guy, taking time to drive me home the other night. He didn't need to do that."

"He wanted to make sure you got home okay."

"I-I shouldn't have been so careless. It's not me." Then she glanced at the flowers in her hands as if she'd forgotten they were there. "Oh, here," she said, offering Jillian the flowers. "Please accept my apology and, really, there's nothing to worry about. I was having—"

"A moment?"

"Yeah, seems like I'm having a lot of those lately. I think it's time I made some decisions about my life." She shrugged her shoulders hard, dismissing the subject.

"Well, thank you for the flowers, Dakota. They're beautiful and if ever you want to talk, please come see me. I know we don't know each other well, but I'm willing to listen and sometimes an objective opinion can really help."

"Thanks," she said, nodding, a glow entering her eyes. "I appreciate that." Next, she did a three-sixty around the stop, perusing all the renovations. "This place is shaping up nicely. I kinda can't wait to see your merchandise."

Really? Jillian didn't usually judge a book by its cover, but the tomboyish female didn't seem the type to go in for fancy lingerie. Although, she'd seen how she'd dressed the day she'd bid on Jack and then again at the engagement party and she'd been stunning. "And I can't wait to show it to you. I will definitely invite you to my soft grand opening in a few weeks."

"Thank you. I'd love that."

"I'd love it too."

"What's with all this love going around?" Brett walked in, interrupting them by standing close, hands on hips, his tool belt wrapped below his waist gunslinger style. He was a confident guy, without being a jerk. Jillian was just learning how to make that distinction. "You got some leftover for me, Day?"

She chuckled. "In your dreams, Brett Collier."

"May Day, you break my heart." He crossed his hand over his heart.

She shooed him away as if he was a pesky bug. "Get yourself back to work. And don't you be telling the world my middle name now."

"Yeah, I know. It's our little secret."

Dakota rolled her eyes. "To think I have the misfortune of being his neighbor," she said good-naturedly to Jillian.

"Yeah, but I'm handy to have around," he said, pointing the butt end of his hammer at her, before walking off.

"You two are friends?" Jillian asked.

Dakota kept her eyes on him until he settled himself by a shelf and began pounding nails. "Neighbors." And then she admitted, "And friends, I guess."

"Well, he was able to put a smile on your face."

"Yeah, Brett makes me laugh. Most days, anyway."

"A man who can do that, is worth his weight." And suddenly Jack's grinning face appeared in her mind.

By late afternoon, Jillian finished up her work and it gave her a renewed sense of pride to lock the doors on her establishment. It never got old, the feeling of accomplishment, the thrill of seeing a new shop come to life and be nurtured to success. No matter how many stores, no matter how many problems, she always came away with a swell of emotion lodging in her throat that she'd built this tiny-sized empire on her own. It was the one thing she had to hold on to, the one thing that brought her happiness.

Unconditionally.

She clicked the lock on her little red sports car and climbed in. It really wasn't a practical car at all and she'd thought about replacing it with something roomier, something that made sense, but tonight she didn't care. She loved this car and what it signified; her independence, her success. She started the engine and pulled out of her parking spot, driving slowly along the streets of Hope Wells as though she didn't have a care in the world. She wasn't especially eager to get home, or rather to get to Jack's home and into the role of pretend fiancée.

But Hope Wells was a small town and even though she'd taken the longest route possible, too soon she found herself sitting in Jack's driveway. She killed the engine, took a big breath and got out, clicking the door locked.

She entered the house she'd share with Jack for the next year, tossed her purse on the sofa, and headed directly to the kitchen. She saw the blood-soaked dish towel first, laying on the white counter tiles and followed the path of crimson drops until she spotted Jack clutching his gut slouched over the kitchen sink.

Her throat hitched as she rushed over to him. "Jack, you're bleeding."

Chapter Nine

"I'M FINE, JILL-IAN." Jack insisted as she tucked herself under his arm, propping him the best she could and gently guiding him into his bedroom.

"You'll be finer once I get you down on this bed."

"Ain't that the truth, sweetheart," he muttered, a sad attempt at levity.

His face was cut just under his right eye and blood continued to seep from that wound. His mouth was swollen and bruises were turning color right before her eyes. His right hand was bloodied at the knuckles and there were bloodstains over the top half of his uniform.

Jillian bit her lip, her stomach twisting, seeing Jack injured like this. He was a lawman and with that job came risk, but Hope Wells wasn't exactly a crime haven and the dangers of Jack's job had never occurred to her before.

She helped lower him down, his head hitting a nice soft pillow. "What happened, Jack?"

"I was jumped from behind and worked over pretty darn good."

"Oh, God."

"You should see the other guys." The swelling on his mouth made for a pretty grim smile. Leave it to Jack to joke, even about something this gruesome.

"Guys? As in plural?"

He gave his head a slight nod. "Three."

Jillian froze, her heart stilled for a moment, unable to comprehend Jack being beaten up by three thugs. This kind of thing wasn't supposed to happen in Hope Wells. "Hold on a sec," she said. "I'll be right back."

Jillian quickly gathered the supplies she needed from the bathroom and returned with antiseptic, gauze, water, and towels. She rested her bottom on the side of the bed. "Your shirt is soaked. Do you want me to take it off?"

His brows lifted and the innuendo didn't need qualifying. Quickly, though, he gave her a thoughtful look and sat up. With his help, she removed the shirt carefully, rolled it up into a ball and set it onto the floor. He flopped back onto the bed.

"Who would do this to you?" she asked.

"There were some hangers-on after the rodeo," he said through puffy lips. "We had a run in or two. Could've been them."

"But you're not sure?"

"Not exactly. I called it in as I was driving home."

"You should've gone to the hospital."

He shook his head slowly. "Nothing's broken. Just bruised. I need to file a report tonight."

"You're not going anywhere tonight, Jack," she said softly and waited for an argument that didn't come. Jack closed his eyes and took deep breaths. "Where were you when this happened?" Gently, she dabbed at the cuts under his eyes. He held back a flinch and she gave him credit for trying to minimize the pain he was in for her sake.

"Parking lot behind the flower shop."

"What were you doing there?"

His eyes opened and he made another attempt to smile. "Buying flowers."

"Oh." That really didn't answer her question.

"For you."

"For m-me?" Jillian nearly swallowed her tongue. A dozen questions came to mind but she didn't voice them. She was more concerned about Jack's injuries than wondering why he wanted to bring her flowers. "I'm so sorry this happened."

Tears welled in her eyes and something hot burned its way to her gut. Jack was out buying flowers for her. How could a simple act turn so violent? But she knew. Deep in the pit of her stomach, she really did know. She was a jinx. Jack's bad luck charm. Ever since she'd shown up here, Jack's well-ordered life had taken an unholy turn for the worst.

She shouldn't be here. She shouldn't have come back to Hope Wells. But even though those thoughts seared a path to her brain and screamed at her for involving Jack in her problems, she also knew she had to muster up and see it through. She couldn't let Jack down. If he lost little Beau on her account, she'd never be able to look herself in the mirror.

"Comes with the job," he said lifting one shoulder slightly in a battered shrug.

The blood from his shirt had seeped onto his chest and she dabbed at it. Luckily, there didn't appear to be any gashes anywhere on his torso, though some nasty bruises were starting to turn color. "How are your ribs?"

"I'm breathing fine," he said quietly. "Like I said, nothing's broken."

"And how would you know that for sure?"

"This isn't my first rodeo, babe. I've been in worse fights."

"As a lawman?"

He gave his head a shake and then flinched from the sudden movement. "Not as a lawman. I've had a few punches thrown at me, but nothing like this."

"Then when?"

He paused, as if reluctant to say, and then his eyes met hers and the intensity of his stare ran chills down her spine. "After you left town."

"Oh?"

"I guess, I went through a wild phase, before my daddy reined me in."

Her eyes squeezed closed as memories returned. Her mama had dragged her away to the west coast screaming and kicking and it had been horrible. Jillian resented her, resented the aunt who had taken them in for a short time, resented her life in general. Not that Hope Wells had been dear to her heart, just the opposite, but the thought of being ripped away from Jack and the only stability she'd known came as a big blow.

Northern California might have been known for its clear blue sky days, lush vineyards, sparkling with ripe purple fruit, and coastal cities booming with culture, but for Jillian, living with her aunt and step-uncle meant cold, lonely days and nights where she sobbed herself to sleep. Where she wouldn't make a friend out of sheer stubbornness. Where she could've easily been mistaken as a soul-empty, foot-shuffling cast member of *The Walking Dead*.

But she'd never thought Jack would have it as bad. She never thought Jack would lose himself to disorderly conduct. By nature, he was only a rebel in jest. He wisecracked his way through school, yet everyone knew Jack to be honest and trustworthy and *good*. To the bone.

So this came as a shock to her. "That doesn't sound like you."

"A man gets kicked in the balls, he comes out fightin'. That is, once he can stand erect again." His lips fought for a smile.

"Oh, Jack."

"It's in the past, Jillian. Leave it there."

She would. She had to. She finished cleaning him up, coated antiseptic on his lacerations and bandaged his smaller cuts. Handing him a glass of water, she spilled two extra strength aspirins into his hand.

He stared at them.

"It'll help with the swelling. And… pain." The words struggled from her lips.

Jack looked pretty beat up but, even still, lying in his bed half covered with a sheet, his chest big and broad and bruised, Jillian swallowed down daring any other man to be more appealing. He looked vulnerable, yet intimidating. Weak, yet strong and so jaw-droppingly rugged right now, she had a hard time peeling her eyes away.

After he downed the pills, she took the glass from his hands and set it on the nightstand. "You should rest now."

"It's early."

"Not that early. And you're tired. I can see it in your eyes."

He closed them and her heart lurched at the pain he must be in, the pain he tried hard to hide from her. She wished he would go to the hospital, or at the very least, see a doctor, but his mind was made up and she knew arguing with him tonight would be futile.

"I'll shut off the light and say goodnight," she whispered.

She planted her feet on the ground and rose from the bed just as his right hand snaked out to grab her. She turned to glance at his big hand covering her wrist.

"Don't go." His eyes were open now, clear and beckoning her earnestly. "Stay with me a little while."

"I, uh, you really need to rest. We can't…"

A flicker of amusement lit in his eyes. "You give me too much credit, babe. Doubt I'm in any shape to make you moan right now."

She opened her mouth in a silent oh, and the man actually grinned. "I'm not asking for anything but your company. Until I fall asleep."

Of course he was. She was a fool and a woman with sex on the brain. Not that she wanted to indulge with him because that would only lead to more confusion, but she could definitely lie beside an injured man to give him peace of mind. What he'd gone through tonight couldn't have been easy. Even the mighty Jack Walker needed a little solace and comfort after having three men unfairly thump on him.

"Sure. I can do that"

She shut off the light, kicked off her shoes, and, careful not to disrupt the calm, climbed gently into Jack's bed, fully dressed. Just a second later, he touched her hand, entwining their fingers from under the sheets, sending sweet butterflies to her belly.

"Thank you," he muttered.

But he didn't need to say the words.

She knew.

JILLIAN WOKE UP bathed in warmth, something tickling the

slope of her throat. Not something, *someone*. Jack spooned her, his arm draping over her hip and his lips pressed against her skin, just below her right ear.

"Jack?"

"Hmmm."

"What are you doing?"

"Feeling better?"

Despite herself, she chuckled. "I'm glad."

"Me too," he admitted in a low, rough voice. The rasp did things to her. Hot, wonderful things.

The tiniest sliver of light coming into the room announced dawn was on the horizon. It was early, too early to get out of bed. She'd slept in her clothes but that wasn't as bad as the signal she was sending Jack, not leaving his bed. Last night, she'd kept an eye out for him to make sure he was okay, to make sure he didn't wake up in pain, but she'd had every intention of going to her own room before sleep claimed her.

Now, cocooned in his embrace, she didn't want to move. It felt good, too good, being with him again. Having his body nudged up against hers and sensing his arousal pushed her to the limit of her willpower.

She wanted him. God help her.

His hand began making circles over her belly, his fingers hovering below her navel. She caught her breath before a gasp of pleasure escaped. And then, his lips were on the back of her throat, pressing and releasing soft moist kisses there.

"I'm glad you stayed," he murmured.

"It was an accident."

She felt his smile against her throat. "Too late for excuses."

"Mmm," she replied, agreeing.

"You feel good," he whispered, his hand inching further below her waist.

Spirals of heat swamped her body. "Jack." She protested rather weakly. Actually, it hadn't come out as a protest at all, but more a whispered breath.

This encouraged him and he moved over her. A sharp grunt pushed out of his mouth, probably from the movement, but Jack covered her mouth so quickly, she didn't have time to ask. Instead, he made it clear kissing him was the tonic he needed.

And maybe that was true of her too. She hated seeing him hurt. Hated knowing the big, strong man had been downed in a brutal way, but today, she could make him feel better and suddenly that was what she wanted more than anything.

She turned to face him. His fingers tangled in her hair as he gave her this moment. She met his gaze and his lush dark eyes spoke to her, revealing desire and want and... *trust*. Jack trusted her. He let her see his vulnerable side. He let her see him weakened and injured, claiming no stubborn pride or alpha superiority. He'd been hurt and he'd allowed her to tend him. And now, he was allowing her to see him buck naked.

Even as varying shades of bruises colored his body, he was breathtaking. Her eyes touched on each of his injuries, one by one, willing the pain to go away, hoping his recovery would be easy. She brought her mouth to his again, touching his lips gently, noting how much the swelling had subsided.

"Heal me, Jillian," he whispered between her kisses.

"I plan to." She only took a few seconds to discard her clothes and come back to him on the bed.

This time when he groaned, it was from pleasure. His hands immediately found her hips and he slid them up and down her body, splaying his fingers wide as if to feel as much of her as possible. Then he grazed over her breasts, teasing the globes that so sorely ached for his touch. He cupped them in his hands and applied sweet pressure and the moan escaping her lips was long and low and necessary.

"You're perfect, Jillian," he said, dipping down to bathe one taut nipple with his tongue.

Sensations rifled through her at breakneck speed now and she reached for him, wrapping her arms around his neck, pulling him closer, arching her back. Everything inside her went tight. Tremors and hot anticipation warred to overtake her body, but soon Jack was pulling away from her chest. His mouth making a claim on her lips and his tongue meeting hers in a flirty push-pull that sent shock waves below her waist.

The next thing she knew, Jack was there, one hand slipping below her navel to gently massage the sweet spot, his fingers riding over her sensitive skin, back and forth, over and over. Jillian huffed. Her breaths shortened. Her eyes squeezed shut.

"Shatter for me, babe," Jack said.

Hearing those words coupled with the way he was playing her body so expertly, Jillian couldn't hold back another second. She did as she was told. She shattered. For Jack. Because of Jack. Her lips parted and a whimper of need came out, a plea that rose along the peak of her sanity, threatening to crush all rational thought. She bucked and jerked and Jack persisted, making her cry out louder as she rode the stream of this heightened pleasure.

"I can't," she whispered desperately, the orgasm rocking her.

"You can, sweetheart." Jack rasped, sounding just as turned on as she was.

After she was through, somewhere in the back of her mind, Jillian remembered that *she* was supposed to heal him, not the other way around. But as she opened her eyes to him, he was smiling, a hotly satisfied look on his face that most likely mirrored hers.

"Are you through healing me?" he asked, finding his own wit awfully funny.

"Not even close, buster. Lay down and—"

"Shut up? You got it." The mattress hissed from his weight as he threw himself back, waiting, his eyes latched to hers.

She wasted no time climbing over his hips and straddling him. Careful not to disturb his injuries, she bent to shower kisses on his mouth, chin, jaw, and then lower to the broad breadth of his shoulders. Nimbly, she moved her body down along his legs and, kneeling between them, she gripped the length of his arousal, teasing and taunting him with her mouth and tongue.

His breath caught nosily in his throat. And she lifted her lashes to see the torrent of pleasure on his face, his teeth gritted and a fiercely hungry look in his eyes. She loved pleasing him and making him hers for these few short hours.

It was heaven on Texas earth.

His taste, the salty silky texture of his thick erection began building another wave of heat inside her body. She was lost to it, to him. His hands pushed through her hair, tangling in the locks deliberately as she kept on giving him pleasure, taking some for herself.

He uttered curses which ordinarily would be vile, but blowing out of his mouth only heightened the sensual moment, only made her want to please him even more.

Her tongue wound around him, her mouth covered him one last time before she rose up on her knees and positioned herself. With his hands on her hips as guidance, she met his intense stare, the darkened pupils, the heat between their bodies, the nod of his head once he had protection in place, telling her he was ready. More than ready.

She sank down, onto him, her folds parting to make way for the gloriously thick shaft impaling her. She had it right. *Heaven on Texas earth.* Her eyes slammed shut, allowing her to simply *feel.* And it felt so darn good.

Jillian smiled to herself. Jack brought out the sex kitten in her. But she'd never admit that to a soul. Especially Jack.

His hips rose up to meet her and she lowered down. The union was fierce and powerful and hot... hot... hot.

Beads of perspiration coated Jack's forehead.

Her body blazed.

It was better than great, riding him, setting the pace, watching the combination of sheer joy and wild lust on his face.

"Nothing is better than this." He rasped, his hands gripping her hips, his eyes on the bounce of her breasts, his erection pulsing deep inside her.

It was sex talk, but Jillian had to agree. If they had one thing going for them, it was wild, crazy hot sex.

It wasn't enough to rely on. It would never be enough to sustain them, and Jillian quickly struck those thoughts from her mind. For now, she'd take crazy hot sex. With Jack. Her fiancé. Soon-to-be temporary husband.

Jack bucked, his hips lifting to thrust fully into her. She crashed down against him and the tempo picked up, faster, faster. She rode him hard, harder, and then his low, deep grunts told her he was ready. She didn't need to catch up, she was already there.

His hands dug into her sides, her skin taut under his fingertips as he held her tight and gave her one surging thrust after another. Sensations whirled around in her head, her mind going fuzzy and then her body released, collapsing in mind-blowing spasms of shocking jolts.

A long, deep groan pulled from Jack's mouth, his face contorting as he rode out the storm, his body pulsing, his heartbeats quickening. She watched him as he watched her and together, they met their ultimate completion.

Seconds afterward, Jack fell back onto the bed, taking her along with him. "Your injuries?"

He shook his head. "I can't feel anything right now *but you*, babe. God, you feel good." He pressed kisses to her forehead, her earlobe, her cheek and then, with a finger under her chin, positioned her head so that he could kiss her mouth senseless.

She curled her arms behind his neck. "So then I healed you?"

"I'm not sure I want to be healed. Kinda nice having you *look after* me this way."

She chuckled. "Part of my charm."

"Hell, yeah. Don't I know it."

"But are you really feeling better, Jack? I mean those bruises on your chest are starting to look really nasty." Gingerly, she placed one fingertip on the worst of the bruises.

"I'll heal in time, don't you worry about me."

But she did. Too much. She cared about Jack. More than she should.

More than was smart.

Or safe.

JACK ARRANGED TO pick up Beau Riley from his foster care home hours after leaving Jillian in his bed. It was the boy's first day of school and he didn't want to miss any of Beau's firsts. The astute kid immediately noticed the cuts on Jack's face and since his uniform covered the rest of his injuries, he fibbed, telling Beau he'd been clumsy as an ox falling over a pile of bricks in his side yard, garnering a relieved smile from the boy.

"Got your backpack all set?" he asked Beau as they drove toward McGowan Elementary School.

John P. McGowan had founded the town years back, owning most of the surrounding land too, and had eventually portioned it off to sell to ranchers. The man had been arthritic and had discovered the swirling warm waters of Wishing Wells somewhat helped heal him. He named the town after the wells and the hope he'd had for the future. Hope Wells had intriguing history up the ying-yang and Jack hoped to share that history with Beau one day.

Beau nodded. "I think. Mrs. Weston packed me a lunch. We went shopping for school supplies. I got new pencils, crayons." The boy shrugged. "Stuff like that." His shoulders slouched; he appeared a little nervous but was trying his best to conceal it.

"Hey, and remember I'm picking you up today. After school, we'll go to the park and play catch. I'll try not to fall over my own feet."

"Okay," he said, his voice a little bit off. "Will Jillian be there?"

Jack immediately flashed an image of Jillian saying goodbye to him this morning wearing next to nothing. He'd had a hard time leaving her. Had an even harder time not letting thoughts of her consume all of his morning. He was in so much trouble. He had it bad for her. Really, really bad.

"Uh, do you want her to come to the park?"

"She's nice," Beau said.

"Yeah, she is. I'll ask her, but I can't promise she'll be able to."

"Okay."

The boy had had so many changes in his life already and starting school was just one more to add to the list. But it wasn't unusual for there to be nerves on the first day of school. Jack had spoken with Beau's teacher several weeks back. Claire Kelly had given him a few pointers as to what to expect. Because he knew Claire personally, it hadn't been a formal meeting, yet it still felt good to be acting as Beau's parent, getting tips and hints on how to deal with the boy's anxiety.

Jack parked the car in front of the school. Beau was adept at getting himself out of his car seat and together, with Jack's hand on the boy's shoulder, they walked to his classroom.

Before sending him inside, he bent down to face Beau on his level. "I've got something for you," he said. "It's something special my daddy gave me, and I want you to have it."

"What is it?" The boy's eyes peeled wide open and for the first time today, he seemed genuinely excited.

Jack opened his palm and the silver-plated deputy badge shimmered in the sunlight. It was a star-shaped replica of the real deal. "My daddy gave this to me when I was your age. Now, I want you to have it. It'll keep you safe and protected and if you're feeling a bit uncertain about things, just remember the badge is a symbol of courage. Would you like to keep it in your pocket while you're in school, Beau?"

The boy nodded, never taking his eyes off the badge. "Yeah."

Jack dropped the badge into Beau's hand. He lifted it up and studied it with boy-like wonder that Jack recognized from his early days with the badge. Finally, a sweet and happy smile lit Beau's face. The kid deserved to be happy every single day of his life. "Take good care of it for me."

"I will." Beau's eyes shimmered with grateful tears. "Thank you."

"Welcome." Jack kissed Beau's forehead, his heart squeezing tight. "Now, go on and have a good day. Mrs.

Kelly is a fine teacher. I'll see you later, Beau."

Jack waved to Claire and she came to the door to introduce herself to Beau. Jack left then, knowing that the boy was in good hands.

FOUR CORNER PARK was exactly that, a park centered in the heart of Hope Wells, its corners touching the four main streets in town. Located just a few miles from the sheriff's office and Beau's school, the park was refuge to kids seeking a fun time. A baseball diamond took up one corner, while the jungle gym equipment and swings took up the other. In between were walkways, a little pond where ducks landed and took off regularly and enough green grass for soccer or football or kite flying.

Jack sat beside Beau on a park bench made of wood and wrought iron, each sipping from a bottle of cool water. He'd managed to pull off a game of catch without Beau seeing him wince every now and again.

Today at the office, he filed a report about the thugs who'd cornered him. The more he thought about it, the more he believed it wasn't the rodeo jocks that'd suckerpunched him and dragged him behind the building to finish him off in total darkness. Those guys wouldn't have been precise, stealth-like, and undeterred. The rodeo dudes were a rowdy sort and got ornery only after consuming too much alcohol. Jack started an investigation to look into would-be disgruntled felons he'd once put away. After more than ten years on the job, he might've made more enemies than he'd like to think.

"So you liked your teacher?" he asked Beau.

"Yeah, she's pretty nice," Beau said.

"Did you make friends in class?"

Beau lifted a shoulder. "I dunno. I guess."

"It'll get easier. You'll make lots of friends in time."

Beau nodded, but he was focused on something else. Jack followed the path of his gaze until he found Jillian, her hand at her brow, searching for them. Beau jumped from his seat and began waving. Jack stood too and Jillian waved back when she spotted them and headed their way.

"Looks like Jillian made it after all." He shouldn't be so dang pleased about it. But he was smiling on the inside and happy she took time from her day to visit with Beau.

"Hi, you two," Jillian said, a sweetly soft glow on her cheeks as she stopped in front of them. She gave Jack a cursory glance before shifting her attention to the boy. "Beau, are you having a fun day?"

He nodded. "It was my first day of kindergarten."

"And how did you like it?" She was bending, her hands on her knees, making eye contact with him.

"I liked it. But I like coming to the park better."

"Yeah, parks are fun. What have you been doing?"

"Playing catch," he said.

"Now, that does sound like fun." Jillian picked up a kid-sized blue Dallas Cowboys football from the basket of balls Jack brought from home. "Can I play?" Jillian asked.

Beau smiled wide. "Sure. It's okay, isn't it, Jack?" The boy looked up at him for approval and Jack longed for the day when Beau would call him Dad.

"Of course. Jillian can play."

"Why don't you sit this one out, Jack," Jillian said, eyeing his chest.

She must've seen the fatigue on his face, something the boy wouldn't notice. And she wasn't wrong. Nothing had been broken last night, but his ribs were bruised. Running around, bending, and tossing the ball to Beau had reminded him of that. "Sounds like a fine idea. I'll add commentary."

"What's that?" Beau asked, his face contorting.

"It means, he'll cheer us on and then take all three of us out for blueberry smoothies afterward." Jillian's face beamed as she ran backward and then tossed Beau the ball.

Jack laughed. Okay, fair deal.

He'd forgotten how athletic Jillian had been when they were younger. Now, as she wore tight denim jeans, sneakers, and a pink t-shirt that sported the BT logo, he got a glimpse of the woman in action. It seemed her tomboyish ways hadn't changed. She was as feminine as woman could ever be, but she could also tangle with the boys.

She was chuckling and smiling at Beau, commending him when he made a good catch. Beau had joy in his eyes and his sprints to catch the ball were all intended to impress Jillian.

The taste and feel of Jillian stilled hummed through Jack's body. As he studied her having fun playing with Beau, something else hurt in his chest, a different kind of sucker punch, stronger, more potent than the punches landed on him last night and one that he couldn't defend against.

He put his head down, running a hand through his hair, and when he looked up, Beau was facing him, tuckered out, his cheeks pink, his breaths labored. Jillian came to stand beside him.

"Smoothies for everyone," Jack announced. "You've had a big day today, Beau."

Beau smiled, beads of sweat running down his face. "I liked today."

Jillian pulled a tissue from her pocket and gently wiped the boy's face.

As they walked away, Beau took Jack's hand and reached for Jillian's too. Sandwiched in between them, the boy nearly pranced as they headed out of the park. Jack looked over at Jillian, meeting her eyes. "I liked today too."

"Yeah," she said softly, "it doesn't get much better than this."

JILLIAN STOOD BY the stove stirring marinara sauce with a

big wooden spoon. The tomatoes did a gurgling dance in the pot as steam rose up flavoring the air with garlic and basil and olive oil. Those yummy scents filled the kitchen as she sang a country tune along with the radio. Contentment filled her up inside. These past few days had been wonderful and not even Tessa's phone call from earlier in the day had rattled her too much. There'd been a fire at her corporate office in Los Angeles. Luckily, the night security guard making his rounds had shown up half an hour earlier than usual and spotted the blaze before it had gotten out of hand.

Initially, Jillian had been very concerned, but Tessa assured her, it was a minor incident, no one was hurt and actually not a paper in the office had been ruffled. The fire was put out before it really took hold. No one was sure how it got started, but hot weather and drought conditions being what they were meant more fires and problems for the firefighters. A careless flip of a match or cigarette could do great damage.

She'd felt guilty not being there to oversee the damage herself, but Tessa had a lock on the situation and wouldn't hear of Jillian leaving Hope Wells right before her wedding. In just two more days Jillian would be Jack's legal wife.

The sound of the back door opening made her breathless. The jingle of keys, scrape of boots across the floor and the door closing again meant Jack was home. As usual, he wasted no time seeking her out.

"Smells damn good in here." The deep timbre of his

voice called to her, made her giddy, made her want. And before she knew it, he was behind her, pulling her close, nuzzling her neck, kissing her throat. "Evenin', babe."

"Hi." A throaty reply was all she could muster. Just like every other night when he'd first arrived home, it had always taken a few thoughtful moments for her to rein in her emotions.

And she'd been like this ever since that night Jack had been injured. They'd fallen into a routine of having dinner and making love. Every night. Sometimes, the lovemaking came *before* and *after* dinner. And it was always spectacular. Neither one of them had much willpower. They pretty much tore each other's clothes off. She smiled at the memories.

"What?" he asked, pulling her away from the stove and looping his arms around her waist.

"Nothing."

He eyed her, his gaze dark and intense, as if willing her to offer the information, but then let the subject drop. Good thing. She didn't want to divulge how she secretly couldn't wait for him to come home, for him to make love to her.

"How was your day?" she asked.

"Pretty damn good," he said, something shining extra bright in his eyes tonight. And that smile of his. It was killer. It couldn't be he was happy to come home to her, could it? Or was it more than that? "How was yours?"

"Pretty good. Except for the fire."

"There was a fire?"

"Yeah, in my corporate offices in Los Angeles. But it's under control. There's no real damage from what Tessa tells me." She gave him the full length version and then added, "Oh, and the good news is the Hope Wells version of Barely There is almost ready to open. I figure by the end of next week, we'll be ready to go."

"That is good news. You've worked hard, Jillian. You deserve all the success you're gonna have in this town."

"Thanks, but not if the Barker cousins and others like them have anything to say about it."

She hadn't told Jack, but a few other women had commented about the shop. They hadn't been as ardent as the Barker cousins, but they'd gotten their point across.

Bless your heart, but I don't see a market in this town for your store.

God love ya, I hope you're not too disappointed with your sales.

Comments like those had Jillian second-guessing herself but she'd summoned her confidence and tried to think positively. For every one of those naysayers, hopefully there would be ten consumers chomping at the bit to browse and buy.

"No one's gonna pay much attention to them," Jack said. His mouth was moving but his eyes were sharp and focused and fully intent on her. "Don't worry, sweetheart," he said and then reached around to turn the knob off on the stove. The flame died down and soon the sauce would stop bubbling.

"I've been thinking about this all day," he said, his words a mere whisper over her mouth.

And then he kissed her, long and slow and deep. She forgot about the meal and everything else except the way his mouth felt on hers, the way his body molded to hers, the way he took control and made her mind-numbingly crazy.

His erection pushed the barriers of his uniform pants. It was shocking to her how he could get there so quickly and then as if he'd heard her thoughts, he murmured. "I can't even think about you at work or this happens."

A chuckle escaped, a bright sound in the quiet room. Thank goodness, women didn't have that problem when it came to lusty thoughts about men, because Jillian would be doomed with all the daydreams she'd had about Jack.

"Oh, you think it's funny?" he asked, biting at her lower lip. "You might just have to pay for that."

"You're all talk, lawman."

He dipped his tongue into her mouth proving he was much more than talk. Immediately heat swelled and pooled at the apex of her thighs and she made a kittenish sound.

"That's it," he said, as he swooped her up, placing his arms under her knees. "Where?"

They'd made love everywhere in the house, except one. Jillian grinned. "I think I need a bath."

Jack's brows rose and he kissed her again taking long strides to the master bathroom.

"I want bubbles," she said, as she slid out of his arms, her feet planting on the tiled bathroom floor.

The look he gave her said *no way*. She was sure he'd never taken a bubble bath in his life, not even as a kid but, to his credit, he ran the bath water, tossed in some of Jillian's luxurious bubble bath, then turned to her, his eyes blazing hot. "Get naked."

A tremor raced up and down her body, curling her toes and she quickly lost her smile when Jack began unfastening his belt, tossing off his shirt and stripping down to bare skin. God, he was a gorgeous hunk of a man. She got naked very fast, and soon they were standing in front of each other in their birthday suits. Jack reached around to cup her ass, both hands on her cheeks and, before she knew what was happening, he lifted her onto the cool marble counter. "I can't wait for those damn bubbles," he said, taking a nipple into her mouth and making her whimper.

She wrapped her legs around his waist and, with his hands still under her bottom, he brought her closer and claimed her mouth in a fiery kiss. The next thing she knew, Jack was deep inside her, penetrating her walls, lusciously invading her most sensitive skin. Arms about his neck now, she moved and he moved, both thrusting, both seeking the ultimate climax. Jillian braced her hands on the marble, lifting herself higher and Jack pulsed tighter, harder and within seconds both were crying out, both were releasing a powerful, amazing orgasm.

They stayed in each other's arms, panting, waiting for their heartbeats to settle down and moments later Jack whispered into her ear, "I'm ready for that bath now."

She laughed. Jack always amused her. "You first."

"Are you daring me?"

"Of course, big man. Get into the bubbles."

Almost jubilant, he let go of her and climbed in. What was with him? Usually, he'd give her a harder time about something like this.

He looked ridiculous standing in the bubbles, but she wasn't going to say that, not when he was doing this for her. He offered his hand and she took it and stepped into the tub. They sank down together into the warm silky bubbles and discovered how crowded it was. "I've got an idea," Jack said.

She thought his bright idea was to get out and let her go it alone. But he surprised her by spreading his legs wide and making room for her between his thighs. He held her around the waist, his hands dangling dangerously below her navel with the beginnings of his new arousal to her back.

"This could get interesting," he said, an evil hitch in his voice. "Lean back against me and enjoy, sweetheart."

The plump bubbles hid their bodies from view and steamy water soothed and caressed their skin. Jack began to massage her belly, hips and thighs and her eyes closed easily as she absorbed the sensual rubdown.

"Mmm," she murmured.

"Like that?" he asked softly, his breath fanning her cheek.

"So very much." It was as calming as it was naughty and Jillian reveled in it.

The possessive slide of Jack's hands under the bubbles, the teasing temptation telling her more was to come. She thought she was fully sated, but Jack's expert caresses told her something different.

He was as turned on as she was. His rapidly rising breaths, the emergence of another pulsing erection, and his fingers angling lower and lower still, until finally he parted her inner folds.

She gasped. The touch was mild, in comparison to the last time, but the impact was greater. She dropped her head back against his shoulder completely at his mercy.

He began stroking, stoking the fires deep within her belly. One hand moved up to cup her breast, and tease the aching nipple, while the other continued to drive her totally, beautifully insane. Her climax came hard, Jack holding her tight against him, not allowing her to wiggle free. God, she'd been so wrong. They hadn't done everything imaginable yet, and Jack was more than willing to tutor her with his expertise.

After a moment's rest, she turned around in the tub and simply said, "Your turn."

Jack's pupils darkened again and he gave her the biggest smile.

She would have to make this last. Tomorrow Tessa would arrive and the two of them were staying at 2 Hope Ranch until the wedding.

Chapter Ten

TESSA WAS A genius when it came to hair and makeup. Not even Texas humidity would disturb the uplift atop Jillian's head or the tresses raining down in barrel curls all along her hairline.

Looking at herself in the mirror at Trey and Maddie's place, Jillian was stunned. "Wow. I didn't know my hair could do this."

"Tessa is definitely gifted," Maddie said, coming to stand next to her. They gazed at each other through the mirror's reflection in the privacy of Maddie and Trey's master bedroom. "You look beyond pretty. You're gonna be a special bride."

Tessa set the brush down, unplugged the curling iron, and slapped her makeup case closed. "Maddie's right. You look amazing, even if I say so myself."

"Thank you," Jillian said. The splash of color Tessa applied on her eyelids deepened the hue of her blue eyes making them really pop. "You're both so sweet to do this for me."

"Why wouldn't we? Jack doesn't know how lucky he is

getting you," Tessa said.

"And you're family now, Jillian," Maddie said. "I'm excited to be a part of this wedding and have a partner in crime. I'm outnumbered by Walker men around here. You're evening up the odds."

Jillian smiled warmly at Maddie, but her stomach ached every time Trey or Maddie brought up their new family ties. She felt worse than guilty in deceiving these lovely people. And maybe, her ache also had something to do with the way she felt about Jack. She loved him. There were no more denials in her mind, no more fooling herself. He was the perfect guy. He always had been. She was crazy about him and it only served to make it that much harder when she would have to pack up her belongings and leave town.

"I couldn't do this without either of you." Jillian took Tessa and Maddie's hands, sealing her appreciation in a gentle squeeze. The three of them simultaneously smiled as tears welled in their eyes. Weddings had a way of making a girl feel sentimental. "Thank you both so much."

"You're welcome," both chorused. "No more tears, please. You'll ruin your pretty face."

Maddie dashed over to the bed and began unzipping the garment bag housing her wedding dress. "It's almost time, Jillian."

With her friends' help, Jillian stepped into her gown. Maddie took a step back to get the full picture. "Oh, Jillian, I have to say I had my doubts about this dress," she confessed, "but the fit is perfect and with your hair and makeup, the whole package is really gorgeous."

Tessa applied a tiny flowered tiara-like comb into her hair.

Maddie handed her a simple bouquet of fresh lavender lilies. "You do look like a princess, my friend."

Jillian did a half turn to gaze at her reflection and her heart nearly stopped. She hadn't wanted any of this. The dress, the hairdo, the flowers, but now that it was done, her emotions rallied. "Oh, my," she said softly.

"I know, right?" Tessa said.

Maddie beamed at her. "Jack's gonna lose it when he sees you."

No, he wouldn't. But it was a nice thought anyway.

Maddie glanced at the digital bedside clock. "It's time. Slip into your shoes, Jillian, and we'll escort you to your groom."

It wasn't a long walk to Maddie's gardens where she'd spoken her vows to Trey. They stopped thirty feet from where the ceremony was to take place, Maddie sequestering her behind a tall mesquite tree. Sticking her head out to view the proceedings, Maddie said, "Looks like all the guests have arrived. Jillian, are you ready?"

"I'm ready," Jillian said.

"Remember as soon as the music starts, walk along the path to the arbor."

She held her bouquet tight in her hands, her nerves

bouncing. After leaving Hope Wells as a teen, in a million lifetimes she'd never believed she'd actually marry Sheriff Jack Walker. But today was the day.

"Okay, good luck," Maddie said, shooting her an air kiss. "We'll go take our seats now."

"I'm so happy for you," Tessa said, and another air kiss came her way. "By the way, it looks like your sheriff is already there waiting for you. And OMG, Jillian, he's gorgeous."

"I know," Jillian said, but Tessa was gone and she was alone behind a tree, waiting for her destiny… well, for the next twelve months anyway.

A tremor passed through her. Could she really do this? Could she enter into a fake marriage with Jack? And then little Beau Riley's face flashed in her mind. That sweet boy needed Jack. Before another thought could cross her mind, a rendition of the "Wedding March" piped across the gardens signaling her to begin.

She came out of hiding and slowly took a step, and then another, each stride a little easier than the last, until her white satin pumps reached the beautiful rose petal-laden aisle. Everyone surged to their feet and turned to her. Monty stood beside a smiling Beau. Maddie and Trey, and Tessa were standing together and she saw many of Jack's good friends as well. But when her gaze flowed a little further to Jack standing under a trestle of traveling vines dotted with vibrant flowers, her heart rang out. Dressed in a black tuxedo with wide western lapels, a narrow tie and wearing his Stetson, Jack Walker simply took her breath away.

As she approached, everything blurred as soon as Jack came forward to take her hand. "You look beautiful," he whispered for her ears only. "You okay?"

She nodded, giving him a smile.

He led her to the natural altar and they faced each other as the minister began the ceremony. It was a short service, without fanfare or lengthy verses. The I-dos were spoken solemnly and as she gazed deeply into Jack's eyes, she witnessed his sincerity, his commitment as he spoke his vows. Hers weren't spoken with any less commitment and then the clouds in her head parted and she had a moment of clarity. They could honor each other as man and wife in all ways, for the time they had together. Some real marriages ended in much less than a year's time. And nothing drove that point home more than when Jack put the wedding band on her finger and she in turn did the same. The bands bonded them now, as did the vows. And Jillian knew a moment of true joy.

"I now pronounce you husband and wife. You may kiss your bride."

Jack took her face in his hands and leaned forward to bestow a kiss on her lips. She could always count on Jack to stir her to the very core. This altar kiss was no less potent, and when they finally came up for air gazing into each other's eyes, they were met with great applause. For a small cluster of guests, they certainly made a racket and a half.

"Ladies and gentlemen, it's my pleasure to introduce you to Mr. and Mrs. Jack Walker."

Jack took her hand and squeezed and then both turned to face their guests. They met with teary-eyed faces on Monty and Maddie and Dakota, but little Beau's wasn't among them. He wore the biggest smile. Even Brett Collier had shown up, a last minute invite to the man who was reshaping the bookstore into Jillian's shop. Through the days she and Brett had become friends. Warmth invaded her body from top to bottom at these lovely people.

"Well, Mrs. Walker," Jack said, "shall we?"

Hand-in-hand, they walked down the aisle as husband and wife. No rice was thrown, no bubbles were blown, but the love surrounding them was just as sweet. Jack kept on walking, farther than she thought necessary, past the last chair, past the tree where she'd hidden behind and then when they were well out of earshot and eyeshot, of the guests, Jack took hold of her other hand.

He held both now and stared into her eyes. "You make a beautiful bride, Jillian."

"You look handsome yourself, Jack."

"I just wanted to say th—"

"I know." Jillian touched two fingers to his lips, shutting off the rest of his comment.

She didn't want to hear him thank her. She didn't want to make any more deals or fall into any more deceit. This was her wedding day. It might be the only wedding day she would ever have and she desperately wanted to believe it was real, just for a little while.

"Jack, let's not talk about it. Can we please not talk about it today?"

Uncertainty entered his eyes and his thick, dark lashes shuttered a few times. "Sure thing, sweetheart."

She gave him a small smile and patted his chest. "Good. Now, I think there's some friends waiting to congratulate us." She lifted her dress and stepped away from her groom, leaving him standing there by himself.

And looking a little dumbfounded by her request.

AFTER A LOVELY dinner Maddie and Trey provided, most of the guests wished Jillian and Jack good luck on their marriage and said their farewells. It gave Jack a chance to make good on his promise to Beau. Now, as the sun was taking its last dip on the horizon, he sat atop Trey's gentlest mare and Jack, Trey, and Monty walked beside him as he circled the corral on horseback. The boy's giddy grin could light the sky.

"He's having a good time," Tessa said.

"Yep, Beau might be just be born to it."

"I meant Jack," Tessa said, correcting her.

Jillian laughed. "That too." Who could argue with that?

Jack looked happy, and in his shirt and slacks, minus the tie and jacket with white shirtsleeves rolled up, he was instructing Beau, protecting him, and beaming with pride all at the same time.

"Tessa, tell me you can stay a few more days. You don't have to leave tomorrow."

"Are you forgetting you're on your honeymoon? You don't need a third wheel hanging around."

"We've been *honeymooning* for weeks now, if you know what I mean," Jillian whispered.

Tessa's eyes grew wide. "Lucky girl."

Jillian inhaled a deep breath. "Yeah, that is true." Add that to the list of her might-never-have-agains. No man would ever compare to Jack in the lovemaking department. It was a weird thing for a new bride to think about, but then none of this was conventional. "Stay." She implored Tessa. "Consider it, work. The corporate office is closed for fire damage repairs anyway. And this way, you can help me put the final touches on the shop."

"Really?"

"Yes, you can stay in the cottage. I'm sure Jack wouldn't mind. It's not as if we're taking a formal honeymoon or anything. Jack couldn't get time off."

A slight fib. He'd offered to put in for it, and she'd talked him out of it for many reasons. One, the shop was almost ready to open. Two, Jack really shouldn't be away from Beau at this critical time. And three, going away somewhere remote to be alone with Jack would be incredibly hard, knowing how this would all end.

"Please, Tessa. I really want you to stay a little longer."

"Okay. For a few days."

Jillian clapped her hands together. "Yay!"

Jack glanced over and she met his eyes. Every time she looked at him lately, her silly heart did somersaults.

"I just hope Jack thinks it's as wonderful idea as you do, Jillian."

"I know he will. I've already asked him about it."

"Well then, I guess you have a houseguest."

Jack walked over a few minutes later, holding Beau in his arms. The little guy's head rested peacefully on Jack's chest and Beau gave Jillian a sweetly tired smile.

"Monty is going to take Beau home now." Home, meant return him to his foster home and the people who are temporarily caring for him. Jack never wanted Beau to feel displaced by referring to foster care as anything but home. "He wants to say goodnight to you."

Jillian's heart nearly burst. The little guy, the wedding among friends, Jack being attentive and glorious to her, gave her a glimpse of what her life could've been. She pined for that life now, in this tender moment, and couldn't help wonder if maybe they could've had a fighting chance at a real marriage. Was it too much to hope?

"Goodnight, Beau," she said. "Thank you for coming to our wedding. I'm glad you were here. You did really good on the horse."

"Trey said I can come back again."

"I think that's a great idea, don't you?"

As tired as he was, Beau bobbed his head up and down enthusiastically. "Tomorrow?"

Jack chuckled. "Maybe not tomorrow, buddy. But soon. I promise."

Jillian kissed Beau on the forehead. "Sleep tight, sweet boy."

Unexpectedly, the boy lunged forward, almost out of Jack's grip to give her a kiss on the cheek. "Goodnight, Jillian."

The gesture meant so much to her. How could one little boy break down her defenses even as she warned herself not to get too close?

"The boy's got good taste," Monty said, walking up and ruffling Beau's hair. "Goodnight, Jillian. Tessa, nice meetin' you." A genuine smile wrinkled all of Monty's creases in a very rugged sort of way. There was no doubt where Jack got his good looks. Monty turned to his son, placing a loving hand on Jack's shoulder. "Congratulations, son. I'm happy for both of you."

Monty kissed Jillian too, and then, after Jack transferred Beau into his father's arms, he fist-bumped Beau goodnight. "Take care, Beau. Thanks for being here."

And ten minutes later, after thanking Maddie and Trey a zillion times for going above and beyond, Jillian was in the car with Jack traveling back to town and to the place she now thought of as home. Jack didn't say, "We did it." He didn't say, "I'm one step closer to adopting Beau." He didn't say, "Thank you." Jack caught onto things quickly, and her little request after the ceremony really must've sunk in. He knew Jillian didn't want to hear those things. Not tonight. Not on her wedding night.

Instead, as he drove off 2 Hope Ranch, he simply reached out to slip her hand in his, covering her with all of his warmth and strength. And once they reached Jack's house and parked the car, he continued to hold her hand. At the front door and without a word, he lifted her, one arm under her shoulders, the other under her knees and carried her over the threshold.

He kicked the door shut and was stealth-like as he moved through the rooms of the house to the master bedroom. It was dark, lit only by a sliver of moonlight, and *perfect,* as Jack kissed her soundly on the lips, set her down until her feet hit the floor, and then proceeded to remove her wedding dress.

Through soft words and whispers, between heated kisses, Jack divested his clothes too and without much foreplay or delay, laid her down on the bed, covered her with his beautiful body and consummated their marriage.

THE SOUND OF Jack's whistling rang in her ears this morning, as she drove to work. Earlier today, she'd come out of the bedroom following the scent of freshly brewed coffee to find Jack banging pots and pans in the kitchen, making breakfast. He'd dropped everything the minute he spotted her and kissed her senseless. And shortly after, continued cooking eggs and bacon, whistling some tune she was certain was totally off-key. Now, she couldn't get it out of her head.

She was smiling so hard, Tessa noticed the minute she entered the shop. "Boy, I'm sure glad I stayed at Maddie and Trey's last night," she said, as the door chimes rang out.

Jillian chuckled. No matter how hard she'd tried, she couldn't convince Tessa to come home with them after the wedding. "You could've just as easily stayed at the guesthouse."

"Judging by your expression, I'm glad I didn't. You two together, well, you're downright combustible. Everyone can see it."

"Did you just say *downright*?"

A sheepish grin crossed her features. "Blame it on Trey and Maddie. Being around them is rubbing off." Then Tessa took a full look around the store. "Wow, the shop is shaping up great. I like what you've done with the small amount of space."

"It was a labor of love, I suppose. I guess I want to—"

"Prove yourself to this town? Jillian, you don't need to do that. You've made a name for yourself already—"

"A tarnished name."

"No way. You had no way of knowing what was going on."

"But I should've suspected something. I should've protected myself and my business better." When she'd first arrived in Hope Wells, once the newspapers had brought her situation to light, it hurt to see barely hidden scorn and mistrust on people's faces. To know they were questioning her trustworthiness and integrity. That, above all else, beat her up inside. But now, with this shop, she wanted so desperately to prove all of them wrong.

"Well, you've got a good guy to help protect you now, Jillian. The way he was with Beau yesterday, all I can say is, he's a special man. I'm glad you found your way back to each other. I know it won't be easy, running your business from Hope Wells, but you'll find the balance you need."

Jillian hoped so. So many emotions were holding her hostage, but she clung to the positive ones, the ones that made her feel good about what she was doing. Happiness could never be overrated, not even in the short term.

Jillian and Tessa went over inventory, set out the lingerie, arranged the coffee counter and planned a strategy for the soft grand opening at the end of the week. Just as they were about to close down for lunch the door chimed.

Jillian looked across the shop to see a chunky older woman, the Aunt Bea replica, stepping tentatively inside.

Oh no. Not what she needed today. One of the Barker cousins.

"Hang on, Tessa," she said and walked over to the lady. "Hello. We're not open, but you're more than welcome to browse around," she said politely.

The woman had trouble meeting her eyes. "I know you're not open," she said quietly, taking a full moment to peer at her surroundings and astonishingly appear genuinely intrigued, maybe even impressed. "I came to apologize."

"Apologize?"

"I was rude to you the other day. I don't know if you remember me."

Oh yes, she remembered her. "Go on."

"It's my cousin, Joan. She goads me into things all the time. I'm not making excuses for my behavior, but I just came to say I'm sorry for judging you. I was out of line. I hope you can forgive me for being a foolish ninny."

Jillian blinked. "Well, yes. Of course, I can forgive you. But, I'm confused. Why the sudden change of mind?"

"I remember you as a girl. You had a rough upbringing. I knew your mother for a time too. Tried to help her a few times, but she wasn't having any of it. And, well, Ella, over at the Bluebonnet, was telling me about your shop. She said, I shouldn't judge you, but to come see for myself. That you had things for seniors that are designed for comfort. I guess, I'm curious about that."

"Oh, I see." It was news to Jillian that the woman had known her mother. She didn't recall ever meeting either of the Barker cousins, but she did appreciate her apology.

"I'm Marla Barker, just so you know."

"Well, Marla, thank you for coming by. It means a lot to me that you stopped in."

"It does?"

"Yes, and now that you're here, would you like to see the lingerie I have on hand in my Vintage There Collection?"

"Alright," she said, giving Jillian a pinched smile, as if she didn't know how to react to her graciousness. "Your shop is really nice. Has an elegant feel to it," she said, gathering another eyeful with a quick scan.

So it wasn't the den of immorality she'd originally thought. More baby steps. But Jillian was all about giving second chances. If she hadn't been granted a few in her life, she didn't know where she would've ended up.

Jillian spent a few minutes showing Marla Barker lingerie and robes to keep her warm on a cold night, explaining about the special materials she used and how her designs were meant for added comfort. Marla took it all in, surprising Jillian at how astute and knowledgeable she was about fabrics. She touched the garments with utmost care and a hint of longing entered her eyes. "These are lovely. They'll sell," she announced, as if she was absolutely certain and suddenly Marla Barker looked twenty years younger, her face animated, excitement in her eyes. "The women in Hope Wells will eat them up and you'll sell out in a heartbeat."

Pleasantly surprised at Marla's turnaround, Jillian sent her a warm smile. "I hope you're right. And thank you for the vote of confidence."

"You're welcome and you can take it to the bank. Your prices are in line, not outrageously overpriced like so many high-end stores and your merchandise is topnotch."

Jillian blinked. There was something about Marla Barker that she was beginning to like a whole lot. And it wasn't her compliments that made her think so, but more a feeling Jillian had about her. It took guts and courage to come into the shop and eat humble pie, they way she did, telling Jillian there was much more to Marla than met the eye.

Jillian introduced Marla to Tessa and offered her a cup of espresso, claiming they needed to test out the new coffee apparatus anyway. All three of them sat down for a cup and Marla confessed, "I used to be in sales. I sold handbags in a boutique in Dallas when I was younger. It was a job I did for four straight summers and I just loved it. The people, the excitement of the city. I learned a lot about sales and I was pretty good at it. I sold on commission and I was always a top seller for the company during the time I worked for them. Ah, I really enjoyed it. Always felt a passion for it, but never went back."

"Why not?" Tessa asked.

Marla shrugged a shoulder, a look of regret in her eyes. "My folks. They needed me to stick around Hope Wells. I took over my father's accounting business when he took ill. But that's ancient history now."

"Too bad. You know, I got my start working a summer

job too," Tessa said. "I worked in Hollywood, selling t-shirts on Hollywood Boulevard. Pretty soon I was designing my own and that's when I met Jillian."

Jillian smiled, a crazy thought running through her head. "Marla, did you see the part-time help wanted sign in the front window?"

The woman stopped her coffee cup midway to her mouth. "I noticed it."

Jillian met Tessa's gaze for a moment and her friend gave her a nod. "Want to apply?"

"Me?" Her coffee cup landed in a soft clink on the counter.

"Unless you're enjoying your retirement too much," Jillian added.

Surprise registered on the older woman's face, and excitement twinkled in her eyes. "Hell no," Marla blurted. "And I would love to apply."

A FEW MORNINGS later, Jillian gave Tessa a giant-sized hug, holding her tight to her chest. Her friend's suitcases were all packed and already in the trunk of her rental car. "Tessa, I can't tell you what it meant to me to have you at my wedding. I only wish you could stay longer."

"Me too, Jillian. Next time, I promise to come out for an entire week. By then, you'll be an old married couple."

Jillian smiled, hating the lies more and more each day. "Yeah. I'm gonna hold you to that, my friend."

"I'll call you when I get back to corporate and give you an update on the fire repairs. They should all be done now. I put Randy in charge in my absence and you know what a bulldog he is. He'll make sure the job is done right."

"Thanks. I'm sure it's fine. I trust the team."

"Yeah, because we have an awesome boss."

Jillian hugged her again. "I'm gonna miss you something fierce, as they say in Texas."

Tessa smiled. "Same here. Be sure to say good-bye to Jack for me. And thank him for the hospitality."

"We should've done more. Shown you some of the sights in Hope Wells. Instead, I had you working at the shop with me for days."

"I loved it. Wish I could be here tomorrow for the grand opening. I'm sure it's going to be *amazing*." She sang the last word and Jillian laughed.

"Have a good flight, Tessa. And I'll be commuting back and forth occasionally, so don't think I'm abandoning you in L.A."

They shared one last hug and then Tessa drove off in her rental car. She waved and watched until the car was out of sight. At a loss, she did what she always did when she felt sad or lonely; she drove to her shop to immerse herself in work.

And found Dakota Jennings peering in Barely There's front window.

Jillian parked her car in the back parking spot and then entered the shop and quickly opened the front door. "Hi, Dakota. Are you looking for me?"

Even in jeans and a t-shirt, Dakota always looked beautiful with her large wistful eyes and a long black mane secured in a braid down her back. "Hi Jillian. Yes, I was hoping to speak to you. Is this a good time?"

"Of course. Come in. Would you like a cup of coffee?"

"No thanks. I've had my coffee hours ago. Breakfast comes early on a ranch. Wow, this place is great." Dakota glanced around the shop. "I had some time today, so I thought I'd come by and say hello. Looks like you're ready for the grand opening."

"I am. Now, I just need customers." Dakota followed her into the heart of the shop.

"Only, customers? I saw your sign outside. Do you still need help?"

"Yes, I have room for one more part-time employee. Do you know of someone?"

Dakota fidgeted with the hem of her t-shirt. "I might." She glanced away before meeting Jillian's eyes. "I'm in the market for something new. I'm thinking, I could help out here some nights and weekends. You wouldn't even have to pay me. I'd be like an intern. That is, if you don't think it's all too crazy."

"Dakota, really? I'm surprised to say the least. You've got a solid reputation on the Circle R. I hear you're wonderful with horses. Everyone sings your praises. And Colby would be lost without you."

"He probably would, but he'd never admit it. It wouldn't be in place of my job at the Circle R. It would be in addition to. I just need... a change. I don't have any real sales experience... and I—" She stopped and gave her head a shake. "You know what, forget it. It's a stupid idea."

"I will not forget it." Jillian saw potential in Dakota.

And she also felt her pain, in falling for a guy who was absolutely clueless. But she'd never hire someone for personal reasons. She was sure Dakota Jennings would give her all no matter what job she tackled. Jack had said as much, he really thought highly of Dakota and he was a good judge of character.

A fresh face, along with Marla's expertise would round out her part-time staff. When Tessa was here, they'd interviewed and hired a full-time employee, Marcie Perez as the store manager. Marcie had ample sales experience as a manager and had just recently moved to Hope Wells from Fort Worth.

"The truth is, I really could use your help. And it would be a paying job. Part-time, of course, but you'd be a welcome asset to the shop. And I would love to have you here. You'd have to fill out an application, company rules, and we'll do a short interview, but I think it'll work out fine."

A rosy tint colored her cheeks and her eyes filled with gratitude. "Really. That's great. I promise, I'm a fast learner, even when it doesn't involve dealing with stubborn animals."

"Cattle?"

"Men. Well, one man in particular."

Both giggled. "Day, you're gonna fit in here perfectly. Okay, then. Let's get started."

That evening, Jillian went home a happy camper. She had a full staff in place now, and a new shop that would add dimension to the small town of Hope Wells. Now, if only the opening went well tomorrow, it would be icing on the cake. She entered the house, dropped her purse on the kitchen chair, making note of the mess on the counters and followed the yummy scent of something wonderful sizzling on the grill.

Jack stood with his back to her at the barbeque, yielding a giant fork like it was a machete, poking at two Texas-sized steaks. In a sleeveless black tank, his biceps rippled as he moved and her eyes drifted down to his perfect butt fitted into faded jeans. Bare-footed, tan, hunky, and chill, this was the Jack she liked best.

"Evenin'," he said, without turning from his task.

She hadn't made a sound, yet he knew she was there. So then, it continued to baffle her, how he could've been jumped from behind without even a clue his attackers were there. Usually Jack's instincts were right on.

"Evening to you too, lawman."

She didn't miss the beige tablecloth covering the patio table, or the two place settings, complete with goblets, sparkling with red wine, the side dishes of asparagus and baked potatoes, or the pretty vase they'd received as a wedding gift filled with lush crimson roses.

"What's all this?" she asked as she stood beside him.

"Looks like dinner to me," he said, with that wry grin of his.

"*Just* dinner?"

He put down his BBQ weapon of choice and drew her into his arms. "Not just dinner. This is an advance celebration of your grand opening."

"How sweet."

His hand slid to the base of her neck. "I'm manly enough to take *sweet*."

"Yes, you certainly are."

And then his mouth was on hers, kissing her until flames erupted inside, rivaling the fiery heat searing the T-bones. "Mmm, delicious," she said, coming up for air minutes later.

Jack gave her mouth one more glance, then his gaze lowered to her breasts, amply covered by the blouse she wore, but that didn't seem to deter him. Blatantly he undressed her with his eyes, bringing tingles to her toes.

He placed his hands on her shoulders and set her away from him. "Go. Sit down. I want you to enjoy this dinner. And that's not gonna happen with you looking so damn sexy."

Sexy? She was wearing black jeans and a tucked in white blouse, nothing special or out of the ordinary. She didn't dress this morning thinking she looked like a sex goddess, but that was exactly how Jack was looking at her now.

She smiled inside, despite her outward pout. "Okay, if I have to."

"You do," he said in his lawman voice.

Now, *that* was sexy.

She sat down and sipped wine and, a few minutes later, Jack brought the steaks over.

They dined quietly, Jack devouring his food as he always did and together they consumed an entire bottle of wine. "If you think me hiring Marla Barker was a hoot," she said, slightly tipsy, "you'll never guess who else I hired today."

Jack eyed her over his goblet, taking several way-off guesses and then finally gave up.

"Dakota Jennings is my newest employee."

"No shit?"

"None. She came in today, saying she needed a change and we talked. She's not quitting the ranch or anything, but she's certainly looking for some diversion and maybe a new direction in her life."

"Yeah, Colby's got that poor girl spinning in circles. But I think she'll make a fine employee. That girl is all heart."

"I know, I feel the same way. So I hired her as a part-timer."

"That'll be good for her, but I can't say I'm not surprised. Dakota is one hundred percent tomboy."

"Maybe not so much anymore, Jack."

"Oh, yeah? I bet you were never a tomboy." His eyes blazed hot, devouring her body with the same intensity he'd gobbled up his meal, making her bones melt, her heart stir and her insides quake.

"You know I wasn't. I was more the devil in disguise."

Jack blinked and then rose to offer her his hand, whispering next to her ear, "Show me."

And that was all he needed to say. "Gladly." She led him into the bedroom. "Take a load off," she whispered and gave his chest a gentle push.

He fell easily onto the bed. Immediately his hands went behind his head, in a leisurely pose that contradicted the hunger burning in his eyes. Jillian grabbed three of her favorite Barely There creations, walked into the bathroom and changed into the first one. Jack had been hinting at a fashion show for days now and it was time she gave him one. Modeling her lingerie solely for Jack was a big turn-on. Why hadn't she done this before?

She exited the bathroom in white silk, a skimpy piece accented with lightweight copper studs adorning the material around all edges, even the backside that flowed naturally into the crease of her butt. She grabbed Jack's tan Stetson, plopped it on her head, and pivoted around doing a slow three-hundred and sixty degree turn.

"This one is called, 'Good Girl of the West'," she said softly. "You like?"

Jack sat up. His eyes darkened and he blew a heavy sigh

from his mouth. Cleavage was a given in these designs but Jack's gaze kept drifting to her ass, nearly fully exposed by the thong gracing the center of her thighs.

"Come here." He nearly growled.

"I take that as a yes, lawman." She wagged a finger at him. "You stay put. There's more."

Jillian's heart raced. She loved modeling for Jack. She'd never done this before for a man, and she never would again. But tonight, Jack was her captured audience. Her body began to tremble as she slipped into a black, skintight faux leather off one shoulder design. The piece was strategically slashed in half a dozen places in front and back, revealing lots and lots of skin. It was by far her sexiest piece in her collection.

As she spun slowly around for Jack, she said softly, "This is one is called—"

"Fuck Me?"

She chuckled, shaking her head. "No, but close. It's called, 'Midnight Surprise'."

A sound rumbled from Jack's throat. "Same thing." He grabbed for her, but she stepped back, out of his reach.

"No groping the model. I've got one more to show you."

Jillian scooted back into the bathroom and quickly changed. Having Jack watching her so intensely was making her jittery. Heat began pooling between her thighs.

"Ready?" she asked, holding her breath.

This one wasn't her bestseller. It wasn't the most unique

but it was her very favorite because it was Jack inspired. She stepped into the bedroom and twirled slowly around, the baby doll nightie following her in a circle with the wisps of material finally settling at the crest of her thighs when the circle was complete. The top and bottom hems were made of the softest white man-made fur.

"This is 'Baby Doll Blue'," she announced quietly. "My favorite."

It was how Jack used to describe her big blue eyes. And she wondered if he remembered.

He rose slowly from the bed and walked over to her, his eyes ablaze and knowing. "It's my favorite too." He slipped her hand in his and inched her closer, then brought his lips down on hers for a brief kiss. He tasted deliciously of smooth red merlot. "The only thing I'd love more than you *in* that baby doll, is taking you *out* of it. Is the show over?"

Jillian reached up to run her hands down his face. Evening stubble scraped the base of her palms and she had visions of him gently scraping other parts of her body. "Oh, baby. The show's just beginning."

Jack laughed, lifted her feet off the ground, and spun her around in his arms.

After that, he peeled away her baby doll and she shed him of his clothes. Bodies burned as kisses sent them both up in flames. His hands were on her everywhere, his caresses rousing every single part of her. Naked and in his arms was the headiest place to be and Jack knew exactly what she liked, what she wanted. He was quick to please.

This part of their lives was beyond perfect and in the moment she was his and this big, solid Hercules of a man was hers. And when their bodies joined, it was as familiar as it was new and exciting. It was welcome and right and so very satisfying.

"I can't get enough of you," Jack whispered afterward, his voice rough and a little bit mystified.

This bliss couldn't last and in the back of their minds, they both had to understand that. But, for now, Jillian couldn't get enough of him either.

"Same here, lawman," she admitted.

Then, once they were partially clothed again and breathing normally, Jack announced. "I have cake."

Jillian chuckled. "What kind?"

"Chocolate."

Was there any other kind? "Show me," she said.

And Jack took her hand and led her into the kitchen.

Chapter Eleven

JILLIAN'S GRAND OPENING was going great. She opened her doors at ten a.m. to a rush of customers. She realized many of the ladies of Hope Wells might have been simply curious, and that was alright, but the sales in the first two hours were strong for a soft opening. The atmosphere was open and friendly, inviting people in with pastel balloons and soft background music.

Ella had come by with a platter of her delicious pastries and Jillian offered her customers specialty coffee. Cookies were handed out on trays and water bottles were at the ready too. Marla Barker's employment at the shop brought in many of her cronies, and Vintage There was getting off to a good start. Even Joan, the other Barker cousin had come in and managed a very polite, "You have a nice store here."

It must've killed her to say it and Marla had stood by her side, nodding her head in approval and that had been that.

Marcie was proving to be a well-organized manager. She moved gracefully in the store guiding the customers and explaining about different fabrics.

Jillian stood behind the counter, taking it all in. This was her twentieth store and that in itself was a milestone, but having it here in Hope Wells meant more to her than she'd ever imagined. The acceptance she craved as a young girl was finally being realized, even if she'd used a fake marriage to the town hero to garner it. In time, she hoped, the acceptance would be based on something more.

By two in the afternoon, the crowd was dying down and there was a lull. Her cell phone rang and she glanced at the screen. Jack. She smiled. He'd promised to stop by this afternoon. She couldn't wait for him to see Barely There in action.

She couldn't wait to see Jack, period.

JACK TOOK A lot of grief from his deputies for coming back to work right after getting married. He'd taken the heat, because he'd had no choice. Jillian didn't want a honeymoon. She was too busy working on the opening of Barely There, and she'd been right to refuse him. Lately, he tended to forget their marriage was a fraud. Jillian had come to this town for one purpose and one purpose only, to get her company back on track.

Still the guys razzed him about leaving a gorgeous new wife at home, and the female officers only shook their heads at him, as if to say, *you dumbshit*, every woman secretly wanted to be whisked away by her new husband.

Jack couldn't win, but he found himself grinning like a fool anyway. He and Jillian clicked. How fortunate he was to come home to a woman at night that was happy to model sexy lingerie for him.

"You daydreaming, boy?" Jack glanced up to find his father walking into his office.

"Hell, no, I'm not daydreaming." Jack had a pile of folders on his desk, an official report on his lap and a shitload of work to do.

"Could've fooled me. Did you tell her yet?"

"Damn it, Dad," Jack said, gritting his teeth and lowering his voice. "Close the door."

Monty immediately spun around and closed the door, but didn't bother with the blinds. Nobody in the department ever shut them, unless what was being discussed was top, top secret. Which wasn't ever the case in Hope Wells.

"You didn't, did you?" Monty eyed him suspiciously.

Jack ran a hand down his face. "No, I haven't told her. I haven't told a soul. You're the only one who knows."

"What is it with you, son? You've got life by the balls right now. You're getting everything you want."

Was he? He wasn't so sure about that.

"I have my own suspicions about why you haven't told Jillian about the adoption going through."

"Dad, I told you already, the paperwork hasn't come through yet. I'm not gonna say a word until that happens, just in case there's a snag. I don't want to risk Beau getting disappointed."

"Bull. The paperwork is a formality. You're scared."

That hit a nerve. He sat up in his seat. "I'm not scared."

"Then why haven't you told her? Or Beau. It's been a week."

"I just told you why. Now, go away."

"You're afraid she's gonna walk out on you again, aren't you? You gotta give Jillian more credit than that. She's—"

"I know what the hell she is." He lowered his voice. "She's my fake wife, Dad. I made a deal with her, remember?"

"Why the hell don't you admit that you love that woman? Damn, it's as plain as that there badge on your chest and everybody but you can see it."

"I'd be an idiot to fall for Jillian Lane again. She's out of my pay grade, Dad. What we have is a bargain, plain and simple."

Monty shook his head. "You don't believe that anymore than I do."

Jack sighed.

Monty watched him carefully and then finally changed the subject. "You got any leads on who pounced on you the other night?"

"I've pretty much nailed down who didn't jump me. But I've got a hunch about something and I'm checking into it."

"Assaulting an officer like that, it's gotta be someone with a vendetta. Someone sending a message. You watch your back, son."

"The team's working on it. We'll find out in due time."

"Alright, I gotta get going. Have a physical exam this afternoon. You be sure to give that pretty wife of yours a kiss from Monty. And think about telling her the truth, Jack. She won't run."

"Out," he said, shaking his head in total defeat and pointing to the door.

Jack fumbled his way through the rest of the day, his concentration level at an all time low. As much as he hated to admit it, his father was right. He owed Beau the truth. And Jillian too.

He'd been over the moon when he found out he'd been granted the adoption, but nothing was legal until the papers came through. That much was true and his fears regarding Beau's future had been put to rest. He could be Beau's dad now.

He'd received the news two days before the wedding and planned on telling Jillian, he really had. But something stopped him, something that came from the pit of his stomach.

Then after the wedding ceremony at 2 Hope when he'd pulled her aside to talk to her, she didn't want to hear anything regarding their deal. He wasn't sure why, other than maybe she wanted the day to seem real. A woman's wedding day, shouldn't be wrought with subterfuge and lies. He got that, so he'd kept the news to himself and thought it best to wait until the papers were delivered.

Deputy Peterson popped his head inside the door. "Sheriff, the mayor is on line one. And fair warning, he's got his panties in a knot about something."

Jack sighed and glanced at his watch. "Fine. Thanks, Charlie."

He leaned over to pick up his phone and greeted the mayor. Two minutes after listening to the mayor go off about his reelection bid being undermined, rising crime in the county, and the failing new ordinances, he called an emergency meeting. "Now, Morris?" Jack asked.

"Yes, Jack. I know it's near the end of the day, but we need this meeting ASAP."

He needed the meeting. Jack needed to pick up Beau from school today and take him over to the Barely There grand opening. They both wanted to show Jillian their support. "Okay, let me rearrange some things, and I'll get back to you."

He hung up the phone and immediately dialed Jillian's number. When she picked up, he asked, "Hey, babe, how's it going?"

"Better than I hoped. It's turning out to be a great day. When are you coming?"

"Uh, that's why I'm calling. I've got this meeting with the mayor that can't be avoided. The thing is, I need someone to pick up Beau from school. He's expecting me and excited to see you. Do you think you can you tear yourself away for a few minutes to get him?"

"Of course. Things are slow right now, and I've got Marla and Marcie here to hold down the fort. I'll bring Beau to the shop and he'll have a ball. I've got balloons and cookies."

"The magic words. Can you stop by the office to trade cars? You know how to work the car seat, right?"

"Yes, I do."

"Okay, great. I'll leave my keys in my office. And after my meeting I'll come by the store."

"It's a deal, lawman. Don't worry about a thing and I'll see you later."

Don't worry about a thing.

Tremors took over Jillian's body as she sat in the hospital emergency waiting room, those words pounding in her skull over and over. When she'd told Jack not to worry about a thing, she'd meant it. She'd had every intention of following through, of taking good care of Beau in Jack's absence, of seeing him safely back to her shop. Now, that poor boy lay in a hospital bed, having tests done to make sure he didn't have a concussion or worse.

Tears spilled down her cheeks. She stood up, unable to sit another minute, her nerves raw from the agony of waiting, of not knowing. For the second time in Beau's young life, he'd been carted away in an ambulance.

Jack's booming voice startled her and she rose, finding him down the hall at the nurse's station. "I need to see my son immediately. Where is he?"

The nurse asked him to wait and when he spotted Jillian, he marched over to her, his steps sharp thuds on the hospital tile. "What the hell happened, Jillian? Where's Beau?"

She cringed. He couldn't make her feel any worse than she already did. "I'm so sorry, Jack. I'm so, so sorry."

He took hold of her arms, his teeth clenched. "Tell me what happened."

On a shaky breath, she started from the beginning and as she spoke, he released the pressure on her arms. "I picked Beau up from school and e-everything was fine. We went to the shop and he had some c-cookies. But then, he said he wanted a blue balloon and the only one left was outside the front of the shop, tied to a lamppost. I walked out there with him," she said, trembling again, reliving the memory. Tears dripped down her face. "I swear I only turned my back on him for a few seconds and then, wham, some teenager on a bike c-came barreling down the sidewalk, hit a bump, and lost control of the bike. Beau was in his path and got knocked down."

His face pinched tight and hard accusing eyes flickered her way. "How could you let this happen?"

"I, uh, I'm so sorry, Jack. I know it's my fault. I should've gotten the balloon for him. I should've been more aware…" Jillian's heart ached seeing the little boy spread out on the concrete that way, unconscious for a short time. She'd sent up a string of prayers while all kinds of frightening scenarios played out in her head.

"How long was he out?" Jack asked.

"Just a few seconds. He came to right away looking sort of dazed."

"But he hit his head pretty hard?"

"I don't know for sure. Oh, Jack, I've been praying…"

Jack's shoulders trembled and he began shaking his head, muttering, "Damn it. Damn it."

She'd never seen Jack like this, not even when he'd been beaten up. He'd never fallen apart like this before.

The doctor came out of the triage exam room, and spoke directly to Jack. "Sheriff Walker? I'm Dr. Rodgers. I understand you're the boy's adoptive father, is that right?"

"Yes, ma'am I am, as of a week ago. How is he?"

The woman smiled. "He's got one heck of a headache, but he's going to be fine. I suggest because of his age, that we keep him overnight for observation. It looks as if his fall was broken. He sort of got tangled up in the front wheel as the bicycle hit him and so the trauma to his head is minimal. He didn't hit it directly, thank goodness. We'll still keep an eye out for a concussion, but other than some bruising on his arms and legs, he's in pretty good shape."

Jack blew out a relieved breath. "That's good news."

Jillian just about fainted from gratitude, her nerves strung tight. She hated the thought of seeing little Beau banged up, but it was a whole lot better than dealing with a head injury.

"Can I see him?" Jack asked.

"Yes, of course. He's been asking for you." The doctor turned her attention to Jillian, giving her a sympathetic look. "One visitor at a time, for the moment. You can take turns going in. He'll be moved into a hospital bed on our pediatric floor in an hour or two."

Jillian nodded, her heart thumping like crazy. "Okay," she said to the doctor.

Jack announced, "I'm going in first."

"Of course."

Jack immediately entered Beau's exam room.

On trembling legs, she took a seat before she fell down and thanked God the boy was going to be fine. What a failure she was. She'd let Beau down. And Jack too. He'd trusted her with the boy, and not half an hour had gone by before Beau was run down by an out of control biker.

There was no excuse for it. She was responsible for Beau's injuries. And even if she hadn't thought so, the expression on Jack's face when he'd confronted her was proof enough.

As she was sitting there, beating herself up in a dozen different ways, going over everything that had happened in her mind, suddenly Jack's words popped into her head. Jack had declared he was Beau's adoptive father as of last week. Wow. She couldn't even process that news right now. Or what it all meant. Why hadn't he told her?

She squeezed her eyes closed. It was all too much to register at the moment.

All she cared about, all that mattered right now was Beau.

JILLIAN SAT IN the dark on Jack's sofa balancing her cell phone in her lap. She watched it, willing it to ring. She'd asked Jack to call her tonight to give her an update on Beau's condition. So far, nothing, and it was nearing nine o'clock.

Once she was finally allowed to see Beau, she was struck by how small and fragile he looked in the hospital bed. Bandages covered his elbows and legs, and a dark bruise under his eye, marred his beautiful young face. She'd bit her lip to keep from spilling tears and had taken his hand. He'd smiled at her, happy to have her in the room. So sweet, so innocent.

Jack hadn't said much to her and his silence unnerved her.

"It isn't your fault," Marla had said to her, suddenly becoming the voice of reason, as they'd waited for the paramedics on the sidewalk.

"Trust me, I have kids," Marcie had added. "They are always getting hurt. Beau will be just fine." But none of it made Jillian feel better. She'd had one job to do, and that was to watch out for Beau until Jack could get there, but she'd blown it.

She wasn't mother material. That was for sure. Any thoughts she'd entertained to the contrary had immediately vanished the second that biker had plowed into Beau. Jillian was at fault. She was to blame. She was Jack's jinx and she always had been. She'd brought him down so many times, but this was the worst, the absolute worst of them all.

Her cell finally rang and she jumped to answer it. "Jack?"

The voice on the other end chuckled in an eerie tone. "Expecting your loser of a husband? Guess what? It's not him. He got lucky the other night. But his luck will run out one day. Just like yours."

A frigid chill gripped her. He was referring to Jack's beating. "Who is this?" She didn't recognize the voice. It was obviously masked to disguise his identity. "What do you want?"

"Haven't you noticed how many *accidents* are happening around you?"

Jillian gasped. She couldn't swallow. Couldn't breathe. The cryptic message stunned her and her eyes began blinking. "W-what?"

"Get used to it."

Click. The phone went dead. Jillian trembled so fiercely, her cell phone stumbled out of her hands and fell to the floor. She stared at it a moment, frozen in fear and then her body began shaking uncontrollably. Had that little boy been purposely hurt? Oh God, what if Beau had been a target and not just an innocent bystander? But who would do such a thing to a child? And what about Jack's mysterious attackers? Was it all related?

Her head ached as she sent up mental prayers. *No, no, no. Not Beau. Not Jack. Please, God, keep them safe.*

She bounded up, suddenly hyperaware of her surroundings, of the darkness. Immediately she turned on all the lights in the house, so very afraid. She needed to warn Jack about the threats. He was sleeping in Beau's hospital room, watching over him tonight. Trembling, she called Jack's phone number and it went straight to voicemail. He was probably asleep by now too. Even so, she blistered off a quick message and then dialed Monty's number. He'd know what to do.

And once he picked up, she said, "Thank goodness, I reached you."

She rushed Monty a quick explanation and when she was through, she was completely out of breath.

"Make sure all your doors are locked," Monty said. "Hang on, Jillian. I'll be right over."

She'd checked all the locks when she'd turned on every single light in the house. Relieved that Monty was on his way, she dialed Tessa's number, needing to hear her friend's voice.

"Oh, man, Jillian. You must have mental telepathy. I was just about to call you. I'm so sorry, but there's been a break-in at corporate. The place was ransacked, computers busted, windows broken and paper files tossed all over the ground. I just got here and the office is a holy mess. The police don't think it's a robbery. Nothing seems to be stolen."

The news sobered her and she stilled her trembling. "Tessa, I'll tell you later why I called, but right now, please let me speak with the officer in charge."

Jillian spoke with an LAPD detective at length, explaining all that had happened today. He'd asked her several questions, especially probing her about whether she'd seen or spoken with her ex-boyfriend, Enrique Vasquez. She told him no. She'd washed her hands of him as soon as she'd found out about his illicit dealings. Caught dead to rights and with Jillian's deposition, a speedy trial had put her once-charming boyfriend in prison for the next five to ten years.

Just as she was ending the call, a sharp rap at the door made her jerk to attention.

"It's me, Monty. Jillian, open up."

Jillian raced to the front door and immediately fell into Monty's arms. He cradled her like a child and for a moment, she felt safe. But it didn't last. Her self-imposed recriminations came pouring out. "It's all my fault, Monty. Everything. That little boy was hurt because of me. Someone crashed into him on the sidewalk deliberately."

Monty walked her further into the house and closed the door, locking it behind him. "No, no, Jillie. Whatever gave you that idea? Beau's accident was a coincidence, is all. The stupid ass kid who crashed into him was Nathan Rivers. His family is as old as dirt around here. I've known that boy all his life. He's crashed his bike so many times in town; I swear it should be revoked. Matter of fact, I'll talk to his folks about that very thing."

"Really? You're not just saying that?"

Monty shook his head and his voice softened. "Now, when have you known me not to speak the truth?"

Jillian filled her lungs, the breath going deep. "Oh, thank goodness."

"Come on. You ready to go the hospital? You need to tell Jack what happened tonight."

Jillian nodded, using her sleeve to wipe away her tears. "Thanks."

THE HALLS ON the pediatric floor were dark and only the blips of the machinery at the nurse's station disturbed the peace. Young patients slept and nurses spoke in hushed tones. Monty traded places with Jack to sit with a sleeping Beau in his room. Jillian leaned against the waiting room wall, facing Jack, and recounted the conversation she'd had tonight with the unknown caller. Jack's eyes were bloodshot, rimmed with red and concern deepened the planes on his rugged face. He listened carefully to her, asked a few questions in full sheriff mode, and then left her to call in the details to his office.

When Jack returned, he leaned a shoulder against the wall facing her and folded his arms across his middle. She could've used a hug from him, but that wasn't happening and she understood why. She had come to town weeks ago and messed up his life.

"You do know that phone call had nothing to do with Beau's accident, right?" Jack asked.

"That's what your father told me. It's true, right?"

"Yes, Jillian," Jack said. "Nathan Rivers is the clumsiest darn kid. He shouldn't be riding his bike on the streets of Hope Wells."

"So then, the fire, you being attacked, the break-in at the corporate office, it all points to me."

"We don't know it's directly related to you."

"But, it's very possible."

Jack nodded, his red-rimmed eyes giving away the truth. He believed it too. Anyone with powers of deduction would come to the same conclusion.

"I'm so sorry about Beau, Jack. I know it's my fault. I know nothing about kids, or raising them. I've been nothing but a jinx to you and I want you to know that I'm very sorry, about everything."

Her tears were gone now. She had her head on straight for the first time since she'd arrived in Hope Wells. And her mind was made up. She wasn't going to impose anymore bad karma on Jack or Beau. If she was in danger of any sort, that was her problem, not his. He shouldn't have to pay for her mistakes.

God, she loved him too much for that.

The town had been right, all those years ago. Jack Walker was too fine a man to shine her shoes. She'd never been enough for him. She wasn't good for him now. Or for Beau. She'd failed on all levels and she wasn't going to give herself a break. This was all on her.

Jack glanced away. He couldn't stand to look at her. He couldn't forgive her. Who could blame him?

"I should go," she said quietly.

He turned to finally face her, searching her eyes for a moment. "I'll have Monty stay with you tonight at the house. You shouldn't be alone."

Still, no hug.

"I'll be fine."

Jack shook his head. "You're scared."

She was. For many reasons and she forced herself to be brave. "A little."

"Monty will drive you home and stay the night, Jillian. Grant me that much peace."

"Oh, uh…"

He'd thrown her off with that, but she'd do anything to breach the gap in his trust. If he wanted Monty to stay at the house, she'd agree.

"Okay, sure. Please give Beau a kiss for me when he wakes up. Goodbye, Jack." She lifted up on tiptoes and brushed a soft kiss to the rough stubble on his cheek. The faint scent of musky aftershave wafted up to her nose, consuming her and reminding her of all that she'd lost tonight.

"Goodnight," he said, turning his back on her to enter Beau's room.

MONTY WAS PACKING a gun and he'd made no bones about telling her she was under his protection and not to worry about a thing. He'd be sleeping in the room next door. He was an old softie at heart when it came to family but, boy, she wouldn't have wanted to come up against him in his old lawman days. He had a reputation for being tough, a no-holds-barred kind of man.

"Have a good night's sleep," he said, shortly after they'd arrived at Jack's house. "If your phone rings again, come and get me, got that?"

"Don't worry, I will." She was grateful to have him here. She didn't want to face the night by herself. "And thank you."

He gave her a nod and sauntered away.

But, she actually wasn't going to sleep right away and a tinge of guilt stabbed at her. In the master bedroom she shared with Jack, she opened her laptop and made a reservation for a flight out first thing tomorrow morning. She needed to go home and the sooner the better. She had employees to console, an office to repair, a business to run and... a heart to mend.

Like that was even possible. Jack Walker was her husband in the eyes of the law, but he was much more than that to her. He was the best man she'd ever known. He was the love of her life and someone that deserved much more than she'd given him.

So, with her mind made up and well after Monty shut off his bedroom light, Jillian quietly pulled out her suitcase from the closet and tossed it on the bed. Slowly, with care and under dim light, she began packing her belongings.

Not a minute later, Monty opened her door without knocking, took a look at her suitcase and shook his head. "You're making a liar outta me, Jillie. I told my son you wouldn't run."

Nothing much could shock her after the fright she had today, but having Monty at her bedroom door did surprise her. How did he hear her? "I'm not running. I have a business in shambles in Los Angeles. I need to get back there."

"Bullfeathers."

The old guy was dear to her heart, and she didn't want to argue the point, but she had to make him see what she was doing was for the best. She continued packing up her bag, rearranging clothes to make them fit. "I'm no good for Jack. I've been nothing but trouble since the first day I came back.

It's killing me to l-leave, Monty." Her voice cracked. She'd been doing fine, feeling noble about her decision, until Monty opened her door and wrecked her with the disappointment on his face. "I'm not good at this. I can't pretend anymore. I'm not a wife or a mother."

"You're both, but you're being too dang stubborn to see it, Jillian."

"I'm not." She glanced at him and shook her head hard, denying his words, even as she so desperately wanted to believe them.

"Jack loves you. So does the boy, even if they don't know it yet."

Oh, how much she wished that were true. But it just plain wasn't. Jack had never told her his feelings. And they'd had plenty of intimate moments when he could have. As far as Beau was concerned, he'd forget about her quickly. He had Jack and Monty, and Maddie and Trey for that matter. A new ready-made family was waiting for him. She was glad about that. Beau was a special little boy and deserved their love.

"No," she said. She turned away from the old man, from the pain and disapproval in his eyes. She couldn't bear to see him hurting. As she set a pair of pants neatly into her suitcase, her eyes blurred. The well had filled up again. "Please, Monty, I don't want to cry anymore."

His dark brown, age-wrinkled eyes softened. "Alright, Jillie. Have it your way."

She bit her lip and put her head down, nodding until she heard the sound of her door clicking shut.

Then the waterworks began anew.

Chapter Twelve

JACK HAD BEEN warned the house would be empty when he brought Beau home this afternoon. He knew this day would come, but he really hadn't thought his marriage to Jillian would only last a little more than a week. He'd been hard on her and now she was gone. She'd blamed herself for Beau's injuries and he hadn't stopped her or made her feel better about it. He'd blamed her too. Yet, he was torn up inside, his gut burning thinking she might be headed into a dangerous situation. An unknown, threatening caller, the fire and a break-in at her main office along with the fact that someone had gone to extremes to attack him, all seemed to send a message that Jillian could be next.

Jack had dreamt of this day for months now, the day he brought Beau home, for good. He thought it'd be the happiest day of his life. He thought nothing could ruin this homecoming. He'd been wrong. He was worried about Jillian. And consumed about her being alone or frightened or hurt.

He couldn't let Beau see his concern. The boy deserved more. It was a fine line he walked today.

"And this will be your bedroom, Beau," Jack said, leading the boy into the room Monty had slept in last night. "We can fix it up anyway you want."

"Really?"

"Yep, really."

Sheer joy rained on Beau's black-and-blued face as he ran over to the bed and threw himself on it. "Oh, boy!"

His excitement pulled at Jack's heart. It was hard to see him covered in bandages, his arms and legs banged up, but Beau didn't seem to notice any of that. He was looking around the room in awe, his eyes twinkling.

Finally, Beau was his son. The paperwork had arrived last night.

"I get to stay here with you, forever and ever?" Beau asked.

Jack smiled. It was the first thing the child had asked after Jack told him the news of the adoption this morning at the hospital. He supposed the boy needed reassurances and he'd repeat it to him a thousand times if it meant easing Beau's mind. "Yep, forever and ever. I'm your father now. You can call me Daddy."

Beau bounded off the bed and ran full speed into his body, hugging him around the waist. "Thank you."

Jack placed his hands on Beau's shoulders, gripping him carefully, but possessively. "Hey, b-buddy." Choked up, he fell to his knees, unable to say more and held onto the boy for a long-drawn-out minute.

For the shortest span of time, they'd been a family by all standards; Jack, Beau, and Jillian. It had seemed perfect, the trio of them skipping off into the sunset. But that wasn't to be. Somehow, he'd have to break the news to Beau in a very tactful way, that he wouldn't be seeing Jillian too much anymore. She'd be back, the note Monty had delivered to him, had said as much. But she didn't say when, or if she'd be coming back to the house. There was finality in her tone, a brush off, in the nicest of ways, claiming that he and Beau belonged together.

Without her, was written between the lines.

After he'd read the note, he'd been hollowed out inside. *She* had never been part of his plan. *She* had never been a factor in the future Jack had wanted for himself and Beau. But even knowing that, repeating it in his head a dozen times didn't really help. And the last line she'd written in her note had hurt him the most.

It's the way it was always meant to be.
Love, Jillian.

Of course she'd come back. She had a new store to oversee. She had to get it off the ground before she moved on. She wasn't coming back for him. Just like, she hadn't come back to Hope Wells initially for him. She'd come to keep her company from going under.

He'd been dumped by a woman he'd known would abandon him at the first sign of trouble. It shouldn't come as a shock. He should've expected it. Now, that part of his heart was closed up good and tight. His mother and then Jolene and now Jillian had all left him. His track record with women was abysmal. It was time to take himself out of the game.

But niggling doubts played out in his head.

You pushed her out.

You didn't give her a chance.

You were harder on her than you've been on anyone else.

Was it true?

He didn't know, but Jillian was still his legal wife and her safety was his responsibility. Thirty minutes later, while Beau rested on the sofa watching a cartoon on the Disney channel, Jack dialed the number the LAPD officer had given him and Officer Wright answered on the first ring. "I was just about to call you, Sheriff Walker."

His heart stopped, panic welling inside. "Do you have news about the case?"

"Yes, as a matter of fact, I do. We have three suspects in custody for the break-in and we're developing a timeline now, regarding your attack and the fire. I think we've got a solid case."

"Who are they?"

"We picked up Juan Carlo Vasquez, younger brother of Enrique. He's a loose cannon, out for revenge for his brother's imprisonment. We've had our eye on him for drug trafficking, and he got a little sloppy last night. Left us enough evidence to make the arrest. He's not talking, but his henchmen are, and we've tied them all to the break-in."

"And Jillian's safe?"

"Yes, sir. In fact, your wife's right here. We're taking her statement. We've had someone watching her since she arrived back in California this morning."

Jack blew out a deep breath. "I'd like to speak to her."

"Sure, I'll put her on the phone. Mrs. Walker, it's your husband."

There was a slight pause and then Jillian said, "Hello Jack. How's Beau?"

"I brought him home a little while ago. He's happy to be here and feeling much better."

"Thank goodness. I've been thinking about him all day."

"How are you holding up?" he asked, the conversation stiff, stilted.

"Better, now that they've made some arrests. I think it's over." She sounded beat, her voice flat.

He was kicking himself inside, wanting to tell her he missed her. Wanting to tell her to come home to her family. Nothing seemed right without her. But he couldn't. It wasn't a matter of pride. It was more. She'd walked out on him twice now. What kind of fool would he be, if he begged her to come home? Their marriage had always been temporary, a fake, a fraud.

"Uh, well, they're waiting for me, Jack. I'd better go." Was he imagining the longing in her voice?

"Yeah, okay. I'm glad you're safe, Jillian. But still, be careful."

"I will. Uh, Jack?"

"What?"

She paused for a few seconds and he held his breath. "Nothing. Good-bye."

When the call ended he ran a hand down his face. At least Jillian was safe. But she wouldn't be coming home to him and his heart was breaking. There was no sense denying it anymore. He'd fallen deeply in love with Jillian Lane Walker, his wife, and now he'd have to live with the pain for the rest of his life.

"Daddy?" The little boy stared up at him and took his hand. "You look sad."

Jack snapped to attention quickly and lifted Beau into his arms, so they were eye to eye. To hear Beau call him Daddy for the first time brightened his mood. "Nah, I'm not sad at all. I'm happy you're here, son. Hey, you want to get some ice cream?"

"Sure! Can we ask Jillian to come too?"

His stomach dipped. "Oh, uh, maybe next time, Beau. Jillian had to go back to California for a while."

"But she's coming home soon, right?"

"I don't know, buddy. Maybe. Hey, after ice cream let's go shopping at the Super Shop and get those new things for your bedroom. Would you like that?"

Beau nodded and hugged him around the neck, squeezing tight. Jack brushed a kiss to the top of his head and they walked out of the house.

An hour later at the store, an ice cream smudged Beau picked out a football themed bedspread from the shelf and Jack already had the sheets in the shopping cart. "Hey, buddy, this lamp is pretty cool." It had a football base that lit up as a nightlight. Jack didn't hesitate to put it into the cart. "Almost done, then we can go home and set all this stuff up."

"I can't wait," Beau said, bouncing a bit in the seat of the shopping cart. "Hey, look, there's Raul from my school!"

Beau waved at the boy and his mother walked over with three children trailing behind her. "Hi, do you know Raul?"

"He's in my class at school," Beau said.

"Oh, nice to meet you. What's your name?"

"Beau."

She looked up at Jack and then at Beau. "I'm Raul's mom, Christy. And these are my other two, Mary Ellen and Josh." The other kids glanced up shyly. The girl, probably four years old, was wearing a cast on her arm, decorated with penned flowers and stickers.

"I'm Jack Walker. I don't think we've ever met. Nice meeting you all."

"Same here, sheriff." She smiled, apparently recognizing him. He was wearing street clothes, but he'd made news lately, thanks to Jillian and just about everyone in town knew what he looked like now. "I suspect we might be seeing you again, I'm the room mother for Raul and Beau's class. What happened to Beau?" she asked, noting his bandages.

"Ah, well, Beau had a bicycle accident the other day. But he's healing up real good."

"So sorry, Beau." Then she nodded in the direction of her daughter. "Mary Ellen broke her wrist falling out of a tree last week. I swear, I only had my back turned for three seconds and before I knew it, the little monkey had climbed up our old oak. Next thing I know, she'd fallen to the ground, holding her wrist." She shrugged. "It all happened so fast. It's hard to watch 'em every second. Even when you do, they manage to find a way to get hurt."

Jack blinked, her words sucker-punching him in the gut.

"You know what I mean?" she was asking.

Jack nodded, his mind racing. The woman had hit a nerve. And woken him up. "Yeah, I do know what you mean."

"Well, I've gotta get this crew home. I'm sure I'll be seeing you again, Beau. Bye for now."

"Yeah, good-bye," Jack said numbly.

Beau waved to his friend as Jack pushed the shopping cart to the checkout line, his heart pumping hard and fast. He hadn't been fair to Jillian. He'd acted like an idiot. He'd been furious at her for not taking better care of Beau, knowing all the while it was killing her.

He'd seen enough through his years as sheriff, to know that accidents happened all the time to kids. They were simply, accidents. Why had he held her to a higher standard, than he held himself? Why hadn't he been more forgiving? She cared about Beau. She hadn't been careless with the boy and Jack had been unduly cruel to her.

She hadn't walked out on him.

Dear God. He'd shoved her away.

And now he had to find a way to fix this mess.

Before it was too late.

"THIS IS SUCH a mess," Jillian told Tessa, the next morning. The police had finally given her the okay to go into her offices, after having retrieved all the evidence they needed. "It's going to take a whole week to get this place up and running again." She glanced around and everywhere her eyes touched found broken glass, computer parts, files cut to shreds. Leather chairs had been slashed, paintings destroyed. It was such an invasion, such a personal attack to her livelihood, that she couldn't stop trembling. "Good thing we have all our files backed up."

"And whose bright idea was that?" Tessa asked.

"Yours. Remind me to give you a big fat raise."

"Duly noted," her friend said. "You know, Jillian, we don't have to fix it all right this minute. You should rest. You've been through a lot these past few days."

"I've got employees, Tessa. And orders to fill. I have obligations."

"I know, but I wasn't talking about that." Tessa gave her a pointed look. "I'm talking about your breakup with Jack."

"What about it?"

Tessa took her hand. "Come with me." When Jillian resisted, Tessa added, "Please."

"Okay, but just for a minute."

Tessa led her to the only room left unscathed, a little employee lounge off the front lobby. "Sit down. I'm making us tea."

The sofa enveloped her as she planted her bottom down. She closed her eyes for a little while, glad Tessa convinced her to take a break. "I have to get back in there soon."

"You can hire a crew to clean this up tomorrow," Tessa said. "There's nothing we can do right now."

"I know. I hate that you're right."

Tessa shoved a cup of raspberry hibiscus tea in her hand. "Drink this."

"You're so bossy today."

"I'm taking care of my friend."

That was one of the reasons she loved Tessa so much. She was like a sister to her. Bossy, sweet, controlling, lovable, and most importantly her friend was in her corner at every turn.

"Sip your tea, Jillian, and tell me what happened with Jack."

"Do I have to?"

"Yes."

Jillian took a gulp of tea before she began. She explained everything from the very beginning, sharing with her the entire truth about why they got married in the first place. She gave her the long version, purging herself, getting it off her chest, and finally being able to speak about it freely. By the time she was through, tears stung her eyes. Tessa simply took her hand and squeezed. She didn't judge, that was another reason Jillian loved her so much.

"And the worst of it is I found out the adoption went through a short time before the wedding. Jack never told me. He didn't trust me with that bit of good news. I had to learn about it by chance when Jack showed up at the hospital."

"Did you ever ask him why he didn't tell you?"

"No. I never had the chance. But I don't know if I would have. Jack didn't want anything to do with me after Beau got hurt."

"He was scared," Tessa said. "And you do know that men react differently to situations than we do. They don't have a rule book."

Jillian narrowed her eyes. "What does that mean?"

"It's a nice way of saying they can all be jerks at times."

She chuckled. "That's true."

She was beginning to feel better, much more like herself. Keeping secrets didn't set well with her and a mountain of pressure had been released as she revealed the truth to Tessa.

Tessa took the cup out of her hand and looked her

straight in the eyes. "You want to know what I think?"

"You're going to tell me, whether I do or not."

"True. Because you have to hear this. I think I know why Jack didn't tell you about the adoption. I think he *wanted* to marry you. I think that he loves you something crazy and you love him, and you're both being prideful and stubborn, and maybe you've both hurt each other in the past and you were both scared to share your feelings."

"Jack didn't want to marry me."

"Maybe not in the beginning, Jillian. But I think he fell hard for you and he knew if he told you he was granted the adoption without having to marry you that you might've backed out. Think about it. It makes sense. And, honey, I saw the look in his eyes when you walked down the aisle in your pretty princess wedding dress. I heard those vows you spoke to each other. I saw how you two played off each together. The two of you are meant to be together. You owe it to yourself to find out, Jillian."

"Even if I did believe you, I can't do anything about it now. I need to get my company back on its feet."

"A minor setback, Jillian. I've got this. I'll take care of things from this end. You can trust me."

"With my life."

"That's what I'm trying to do. Give you your life back."

Monday night, Jack sat on Beau's bed reading him a bedtime story about a little boy with a pet dinosaur. As soon as Beau's eyes drifted closed, he bent over to kiss him on the forehead, tuck his blanket under his chin, and shut off his new football light. He tiptoed out of Beau's room and came face to face with his father.

"You're doing the right thing, son."

Jack couldn't agree more. "Beau knows you'll be taking him to school in the morning. I should be back, one way or another in time to pick him up. If there's any delay—"

"I know, I know. I'm on standby. I'll be happy to pick up my grandson," Monty said, pride beaming in his eyes. Adopting Beau made his father a grandpa and Monty loved his new role.

"I'd wish you luck, but you've already got it. Have a safe trip, son. Bring that girl back to us."

"I'll do my best, Dad. You sure, me surprising her is a good idea?"

"I'm sure. Women like to be swept off their feet."

"I might have to do a lot of sweeping."

His dad slapped him on the back. "You do what you have to and don't take no for an answer."

If only he was as sure as his father was that Jillian would give him another chance. If only he had his father's confidence, but if Jack didn't at least try to plead his case, he'd be sorry the rest of his life. He'd come to the conclusion that Jillian was worth more than his pride. She was worth everything.

Jack tossed his overnight bag into his SUV and revved up the engine.

"Here goes nothing," he muttered as he made his way to the highway, heading toward the airport. He had no idea what he'd say to Jillian once he finally reached her. He wouldn't rehearse anything. He'd been told to speak the truth, to speak from the heart. How had his dad become such an expert on relationships, anyway?

He was halfway to the airport, the radio blasting, his car pushing a tad over the speed limit to make his flight on time. And then he spotted something as he whizzed by.

A cherry red sports car parked along the side of the road.

"What the—" He slowed to a stop and, because the road was empty, put his car in reverse and backed all the way up. Taking a flashlight out of his glove compartment, Jack shined a light on the car. There was no mistaking it.

Jack got out of his car. With flashlight in hand, he gave the sports car a good checking over before setting his sights on the town's most noteworthy attraction, Wishing Wells, not fifty feet away. His heart thumping, he approached and the sound of water lapping, brought fresh memories of the last time he'd been here. He hopped the fence easily, his inner lawman telling him to proceed with caution. But Jack wasn't much listening to his inner lawman tonight.

"That better be you, Sheriff Walker."

The sound of Jillian's voice sent sweet chills through his

body. "You expecting someone else?" God, that woman made him happy. Crazy, but happy.

"I don't want anyone but you."

That brought a smile to his face, even before he got a glimpse of her. Now that he was close, he beamed light on the Wells and saw her submerged in the warm waters, her blonde hair atop her head in some sort of wispy bun. "Trespassing again, Jillian?"

"Yeah, I was hoping to get arrested. By my husband."

Jack drank in the sight of her. God, how he loved her. "Seriously, babe. What are you doing here? After what you've been through, you shouldn't be alone, in the dark."

"I knew you'd find me. I called the house and your dad told me you'd be passing by here."

"And you knew I'd stop?"

"You're a lawman, nosy by nature."

He moved in on her, shaking his head. "Why'd you come back?"

"Not for my company. Not for any other reason. But you."

She met his eyes and he saw the truth there. The undeniable beautiful truth. And then he caught a flash of red. "What are you wearing under there?"

"Guess."

"I have no clue."

"Valentine Vamp."

Ah, yeah. He remembered that sexy crimson thong that

blew his mind when she'd shown up at his front door the first time. "Isn't that how we got into all this trouble in the first place?"

"I was hoping to jar your memory. So why were you coming to L.A?"

Jack shook his head. "Uh-uh. I'm not talking until you come on out of there."

"Why don't you come in? The water's nice and warm. And you can make a wish."

"I've done my share of wishing, Jillian. Listen, I've got a lot to say to you, but first, give me your left hand."

"Why? You going to cuff me?"

Jack grinned. "Something like that."

Jillian stared at her left hand beginning to prune up and Jack took hold of it and slipped her wedding ring off her finger. "I should've never given you this," he said, shaking his head. When he looked into Jillian's eyes, they were tearing up. "Hold on, babe. That's not what I meant."

Quickly, he dipped into his pocket and pulled out his grandmother's diamond ring. "This is the ring that belongs on your finger, Jillian. It's a piece of my family, a piece of me, and now it belongs to you." He held her hand reverently and gently guided the ring into position.

"Oh, Jack. You had me scared for a second."

"I guess we're good at scaring each other."

She lifted her hand, admiring the ring that meant so much more than diamonds and gold. It meant forever. "It's beautiful, Jack."

"It's important to me and it's fitting you should wear it, Jillian."

She gave him a dewy-eyed smile that warmed all the cold places in his heart. "Thank you."

Jack stared at his stunning wife sitting comfortably in the waters. He could hardly believe he'd almost blown it with her. It seemed they needed two chances to find their happiness, but he was fearless now, knowing in his heart that this was the right choice for him, the only choice.

"If you're not coming out, I'm coming in." He unbuttoned his shirt, undid his belt buckle, kicked off his boots and jumped into the wells, splashing Jillian as he came up, shaking his head.

They laughed and he took her into his arms. "I'm crazy in love with you, Jillian. I want you back. As my real wife. I want you and me and Beau to be a family. And, before you say anything, I want to apologize for blaming you about the bicycle accident. It was wrong of me to condemn you that way. It wasn't your fault. Accidents happen all the time, and sometimes there isn't any way to prevent them. Can you forgive me?"

"Tessa said you were being a jerk."

"Tessa?"

"Yes, but don't hold it against her, she was defending you. She also convinced me to come back home. So yes, I forgive you. And Jack, I would die before letting anything happen to Beau."

"You love him too?"

"I do. It's not hard to love that sweet boy. I missed him. I missed you. And I'm proud to wear your grandmother's ring. I'll try to do it justice as your wife."

Jack's heart was ready to burst. But he had more to confess. "Jillian, I don't have a good track record with women. My mom left when I was six years old and it broke my heart. I grew up without a mother. It hurt in ways I can't begin to explain. That's one reason adopting Beau was so important to me. I wanted that boy to have a good father, at least. Like I had. Then years later, Jolene left me to pursue her career. She wanted out of Hope Wells and as I look back at it, we were all wrong for each other. In the back of my mind, I thought you were going to leave me too, for bigger and better things. You'd done that once already."

"Is that why you didn't tell me about the adoption going through?"

He began nodding. "Yeah, if I'm being honest, I thought you'd leave before the wedding and not marry me, if you knew. I'd gotten the verbal okay from the judge and I was over the moon about it, but I ran scared and so I used waiting for the official paperwork to come through as an excuse to hold off telling you. And Beau. You've gotta know how protective I am of that boy."

"I do know, Jack. So am I."

He took her hand and squeezed. "I was falling hard for

you and I didn't want you to back out of our bargain. You see, the problem is, I couldn't really admit that to myself until a few days ago."

"What made you finally see?"

"Missing you, realizing you weren't to blame for Beau's accident. Realizing, we could never be a family without you."

"Oh, Jack. I missed you too. So much. And I wouldn't have backed out, I would've stayed, but after Beau got hurt, I realized I'd been nothing but a jinx to you. Because of me, you almost lost Beau when those racy headlines appeared in the newspaper. You were forced to marry me. And then you were jumped by those awful men, and—"

He touched his fingers to her lips. "Shush, that's in the past now, sweetheart. And you aren't a jinx. I never once thought of you that way. You are the love of my life and I pushed you away. I promise to never do that again. You mean everything to me and I was on my way to—"

"Bring me home?"

"Sweep you off your feet."

Jillian smiled. "You have. You do."

"I'm happy to hear it, sweetheart. I'm crazy about you."

Jillian stared into his eyes. "I may have to commute from time to time until I can arrange to run things from Hope Wells."

"That's fine, sweetheart. We'll deal with it together. Whatever it takes. You'll always have my support."

Jillian sighed, a beautiful hope-filled sound that told him

it was all going to work out. They were meant to be together and no obstacle, whether big or small, could ever shatter the bonds of their love.

"I love you, lawman."

"And I love you."

Jack cupped her beautiful face in his hands and brought his lips to hers, sealing their future with a kiss that brought joy and hope and faith in the warm healing waters of Wishing Wells.

Where sometimes… wishes really do come true.

The End

You'll love the next book in...
The Forever Texan Series

Book 1: *Taming the Texas Cowboy*

Book 2: *Loving the Texas Lawman*

Book 3: *Redeeming the Texas Rancher*

Available now at your favorite online retailer!

More by Charlene Sands

Claim Me, Cowboy
Copper Mountain Rodeo series

Bachelor for Hire
Bachelor Auction Returns series

Available now at your favorite online retailer!

About the Author

Charlene Sands is a USA Today Bestselling author writing sexy contemporary romances and stories set in the Old West. Her stories have been honored with the National Readers Choice Award, the Cataromance Reviewer's Choice Award and she's a double recipient of the Booksellers' Best Award. She was recently honored with Romantic Times Magazine's Best Harlequin Desire of 2014. Charlene is a member of the Orange County Chapter and Los Angeles Chapter of Romance Writers of America.

When not writing, she enjoys great coffee, spending time with her four "princesses", bowling in a woman's league, country music, reading books from her favorite authors and going on movie dates with her "hero" husband.

Sign up for her newsletter at www.charlenesands.com for new releases and special member giveaways.

Thank you for reading
Loving the Texas Lawman

If you enjoyed this book, you can find more from all our great authors at TulePublishing.com, or from your favorite online retailer.